I0780741

Tyler Never Cried

Autism, Advocacy, and the Binder That Held Us Together

By: Jacqueline Guillory

Tyler Never Cried
© 2025 by Jacqueline Guillory
All rights reserved. No part of this publication may be reproduced, stored in a retrieval system, or transmitted in any form or by any means electronic, mechanical, photocopying, recording, or otherwise without the prior written permission of the publisher, except for brief quotations used in reviews or scholarly works.
Published by Happy Harbor Press
[Royse City, Texas] USA
www.happyharborpress.com

Editing and layout by Jacqueline Guillory
Cover design by Happy Harbor Press]
Printed in the United States of America
First Edition October 2025

Content

AUTHOR'S NOTE

When I first started writing this book, I thought I was simply telling my son's story.

But somewhere between the sleepless nights, the binders, the hospital rooms, and the trampoline springs, I realized I was also telling mine.

This book is not a manual, and it isn't polished advocacy language.

It's the truth of one family learning to love loudly in a world that didn't always know how to listen.

It's about the years before hashtags, before sensory rooms, before awareness came and the ones after.

It's about the noise, the paperwork, the laughter, the quiet, and the courage that grew between them.

I hope these pages remind another parent sitting in a waiting room, or anyone who has ever loved someone who sees the world differently, that you are not alone, and that small victories count.

Every smile, every word, every bit of progress is a miracle disguised as an ordinary day.

Thank you for letting me share ours.

May this book find you in the moments when you need a little light, a little fight, and the reminder that love, real love, is never silent.

This story is the journey I had as Tylers mother. Dad is in the book, but I felt his journey with Tyler was his to tell so if he seems absent in parts it is not because he wasn't there or very much a part of Tyler's story, only that his perception and his moments are for him to share not me.

Stepdad also has been a huge and constant part of Tylers life and journey for the last 8 years and is noted periodically in the book.

Tyler had a lot of amazing people come to love him in his life and we welcome them all to share their journeys.

This story took two decades to write

It came from memory, binders and love. Thank you for letting me share this with you.

Two Pink Lines

Loss

The first time I learned how fast a world can fall apart, I was alone in the bathroom of our tiny base townhouse.

Blood lived in the grout no matter how hard I scrubbed. The light over the mirror flickered and hummed; an impatient insect made the room feel slightly off balance. Through the thin wall, Jacob, not yet two, crashed blocks together and hummed in response.

The cramps arrived like a trap snapping shut. Blood followed, fast enough that my body knew before my brain agreed. I gripped the sink, whispering, "No, no, no." There was no one to call; Dad couldn't leave work, and there was nobody I trusted to watch Jacob. So, it was me on the cold tile while my baby played on the other side of the wall.

Pad after pad, the bathroom turned metallic under the blood. Every time Jacob called, "Mama?" I answered, even and steady, like nothing had shifted. He pushed a toy truck under the door (his offering to the animal he sensed in the room), and I bit my lip until I tasted iron, determined not to cry. When the worst finally eased, there were still noodles to stir, a toddler to bathe, and a bedtime to keep. I stood at the stove that night, smiling at Jacob like nothing had happened, my hands shaking over boiling water.

I didn't cry. I couldn't afford to.

I called the nurse line and lied about being calm. "Monitor," she said, like grief could be charted in hourly boxes. "No ER unless you're soaking a pad an hour." I already was, so I said "okay" because dinner was almost done.

I tied the bathroom trash tight so Jacob wouldn't see. I scrubbed the floor until the water ran pink, then clear, then pink again because the body doesn't care about closure. I folded the tiny camo onesie back into the drawer the way you hide a knife, carefully, pointing away.

When I finally sat on the edge of the tub, the tile pulled heat from my legs and left an ache in my bones. The timer on the stove saved the noodles and my secret. Motherhood, even in loss, requires punctuality.

I promised myself I'd cry later, as if later were a room you could enter and close the door behind you. Later I kept moving.

That evening, Dad came home smiling. He scooped Jacob up, covered his cheeks in loud kisses, then crossed the room to me with a grin that lit our dull apartment. His hand slid to my belly; proud, automatic, already a father again. I felt my face split into a smile I didn't mean because I knew Jacob was watching. Inside, the truth roared: there was no baby to touch.

Dad was blissfully unaware. He paused at the exchange, purchasing a tiny onesie, triumphantly raising it like a victory flag. "For the next Marine," he declared. I longed to be shattered. Instead, I nodded, embraced him, and tucked the new onesie away, hidden beneath T-shirts, battling the blast of memories each time we opened that drawer.

In that moment, I uncovered a truth about our marriage and life in uniform: while he might brave the world, I would wage our war. I became the glue holding our pieces together, even on the days when strength felt elusive.

Later that night, once Jacob was peacefully resting and chores were completed, I gathered all my courage. I gently told Dad that my body had failed us. And another heart-wrenching

Control

Dad worked through the loss the only way he knew protocols, checklists, and staying late. The uniform was safe; grief wasn't. We barely spoke about it. Silence felt safer than pressing on the bruise.

Loss taught me an unhelpful skill: how to hold joy with suspicion. How to keep moving while you're bleeding. How to mother while coming apart.

Something old woke up…control. As a teenager, anorexia had made the ground feel steady: numbers, miles, subtraction. Pregnancy swapped units but not instinct. I counted safety now. Caffeine went first. Sugar became pennies to ration. Tuna disappeared because a book said no mercury, and I obeyed. I taped a list to the fridge like scripture: no tuna, no caffeine, deli meat only if microwaved. Do not tempt fate; do not give fate an excuse.

When I wanted coffee, I chewed ice until my jaw ached. Passing the commissary tuna aisle, I didn't look. I told myself it was discipline, but really it was penance. If the universe was going to take something again, it wouldn't be because I broke a rule.

Routine

Months limped by. I patched together routines; Jacob, dishes, perfecting the performance called strength that military wives wear like armor. Our townhouse was drafty; the walls were thin enough to hear our neighbors laugh but not thick enough to ask for help. I was twenty, too young and too tired. On game nights with other young couples, laughter moved around the table like a casserole. When the talk turned to promotions and per diem, someone would ask, "What do you do?" and without fail my answer would elicit the pity-smile that landed soft as a pat. "Oh. You're home with him. That's… nice." I learned to laugh on cue and make a mental after-action report on the walk home: talked too little, apologized twice, mentioned being tired. Next time I'd bring a dip and a story that sounded like a plan. Surely, I could come up with something interesting to say.

Second Test

Then one morning I was back in that bathroom. Same smell, same vent hum. Same shaking hands. Another test.

One line appeared. Then the second; fast, decisive, cruelly familiar. My heart lurched and sank at once. Gratitude wrestled with panic. I pressed the stick against my thigh like steadying plastic could steady a future.

This time would be different. I had followed every rule. I whispered bargains into the mirror: I'll do better, I'll do everything right, just let this one stay. Happiness didn't flood me. Exhaustion did, and underneath it a small, steady plea: please, not another loss.

Work

I'd just landed a miracle, an on-site property manager job with a discounted two-bedroom. Our ticket off base. I practiced being the kind of woman who didn't flinch when a supervisor walked in. I was brisk and reliable; I efficiently kept my maintenance tickets triaged in neat stacks. I wrote names that mattered on a sticky note and tucked it under the phone like vocabulary I could master.

The breakroom smelled like burnt coffee and new carpet glue. I learned the coffee schedule before the software: Miguel at seven, Diane at ten-thirty, both terrible in different ways. When the nausea began stalking me, I mapped bathrooms like exits on a plane. Mint gum until my jaw ached. Knees on tile bargaining with a stomach that didn't negotiate. I learned how long I could vanish without notice (four minutes) and how to wash my hands without meeting my own eyes. "You, okay?" a coworker asked once. I smiled the kind of smile that says, don't touch me or I'll shatter. By the time I admitted I couldn't keep up, the decision had already made itself. Security didn't escort me out; fatigue did.

Without the job's apartment, the math collapsed. His Marine pay alone couldn't cover rent. We could lose the off-base place or split up temporarily until base housing opened again. Diapers, bottles, a second car seat, and another baby are its own economy. The plan looked simple: he'd stay in the barracks or with friends. I'd take Jacob and my belly to family in Florida. We'd save every dollar. We promised to send emails, no texting or cell phones back then. We aimed to meet again with some savings by the time the baby arrived.

Leaving felt like failure. I had promised myself I could hold us together; it would be worth the time apart.

Florida

Florida made sense on paper. Family is nearby. A few months until the baby. A waiting spot on the base housing list.

My "bedroom" was a pallet of blankets beside Jacob's Nemo blanket and sleeping bag. Every toss and turn sent a spike through my hips; the baby sat heavy and low. I listened to Jacob's sleepy hum and told myself this was temporary, only until we could afford to go home.

Days blurred. I tried to give Jacob something normal. We walked to the condo pool where he splashed until his small shoulders turned golden. For brief moments in time, it felt like summer vacation: chlorine, sunscreen, his high laugh bouncing off concrete. Underneath, I was twenty, pregnant, broke, living on someone else's floor.

There was one sure light. Nanny worked at the Pretzel Twister in the mall, and Jacob adored her so fully he renamed her Grandma Pretzel. On slow afternoons we visited. He stood behind the counter, wide-eyed, watching her twist dough into perfect knots. Sometimes he "helped" sweep; sometimes he pressed his fingers to the glass and watched. At home she taught him jacks and marbles on the linoleum, how to dig in the garden, and how to wait while fishing. I'd watch them, his brown shoulders, a Happy Meal toy clenched in his fist, Nanny laughing at his serious questions, and the anxiety slipped away for a few hours. Nanny had always been my safe place. Sitting at her table still felt like armor. Maybe that's where Jacob learned his quiet strength.

The breaking point came wrapped in smoke. I'd asked (gently, I thought) if people could avoid smoking around me. The answer was laughter that didn't feel kind.

"It's not that big a deal," someone said, flicking ash out the slider like smoke doesn't drift back. "Your cousin smoked, and her kids are fine."

"I'm not my cousin," I said, hand on my belly because I had nothing else to hold. "I'm pregnant. I don't want to be around it."

"God, you're so stuck up." A laugh without warmth. "You think you're better than us because you read a book."

"I think I'm trying to keep a baby alive."

"Controlling," someone ruled from the deck.

I swallowed what I wanted to say, carried Jacob to the car and drove back to the condo. There I found sanctuary in what we called our "bedroom" that was our pallet, and lay beside him breathing through stale air, building a different life in my head with windows I could open. I remember thinking, I'd rather struggle in California alone than feel like this again. That night, resolve clicked into place. Temporary or not, this wasn't home. I missed Dad. I even missed the drafty base house. I wanted air, I didn't have to ask permission to breathe.

Return

Eventually, we scraped together enough to return.

Coming back wasn't triumphant; it was crawling. We decided not to wait for a base opening and found a small one-bedroom apartment. It had beige siding, crooked blinds, and the smell of old paint, but when we pulled in, I could breathe. Dad was waiting, awkward and smiling, and Jacob launched at him like the months apart were a nap. We carried in everything we owned: hand-me-down furniture, trash bags of clothes, and one set of pots. It wasn't much, but it was ours. That night, after Jacob proudly made a bed on his borrowed mattress, we all split McNuggets on the floor. Quiet relief. Under one roof again felt like survival. We ate straight from the cartons because the cabinet didn't have plates yet. Jacob fell asleep mid-nugget, cheek glossy with sweet and sour sauce.

The next day I made a game of unpacking: count the spoons, find the lost sock, who can stack the books tallest, and he crowned himself king of Box Mountain. I labeled everything like labels could hold us together: HALL CLOSET, WINTER, KITCHEN, BAKING, BABY. When the apartment finally went quiet, the building still had its own heart: footsteps above, a stairwell door that never latched, the hum of a fridge that had belonged to someone else. I lay awake listening and thought, this is not the life I planned. Then I put my hand on my stomach and told the only truth that mattered: You are welcome here.

Nesting

Nesting became air. Bins labeled with military precision: 0–3-month onesies, ten; sleepers, zipper only; cotton hats. A checklist taped inside the hall closet: socks, lip balm, phone charger, insurance cards, lollipops for Jacob. Wipes stacked like small soldiers. From the outside it probably looked obsessive. From the inside it was oxygen. I cleaned everything until you couldn't tell it was once someone's trash we had collected. Everything was ready for our perfect baby. We were going to make it this time. While I was compulsively packing and unpacking, I would call home. Long distance was unlimited now, and my father's voice gave me peace. He wanted so much for the baby to be born on my granddaddy's birthday. Just two weeks away. I would be exactly 38 weeks pregnant. Jacob made me wait until 41; no way this baby would come when everyone so desperately wanted it. Granddaddy had recently passed, so the wish felt more like a need. Wondering if I could give my family a miracle, I hastily unpacked the bags again, feeling they could be slightly more organized.

Labor

Labor began on October 27, earlier than anyone expected. We lived forty-five minutes from the hospital, had no babysitter, one car, and no cell phones. I called Dad's command to hunt him down and paced the living room while contractions tightened like a vise. Jacob, barely two, followed me, trying to help: fetching his blanket, patting my hand, whispering, "Okay, Mama. Okay."

Dad burst through the door, pulled off duty and wide-eyed. Relief hit, but the chaos didn't soften. Bags weren't packed because I was still organizing and deciding. The car seat wasn't installed because we had just received it. We left in a storm of blankets and wrong shoes, me waddling and grimacing, Jacob clamped onto his stuffed animal like a soldier.

The drive was endless. The hospital smelled like lemon antiseptic and anticipation. A nurse with kind eyes bent rules so Jacob could stay. She walked laps with me while Dad kept watch over our sleeping toddler. "One more lap," she said at each peak, her voice an anchor. She spent most of her 12-hour shift helping me, knowing she might not even see the baby born. The first of many angels placed in our lives.

In the blue hour before morning on October 28 (my grandfather's birthday), Tyler arrived. The kind nurse was able to help deliver and hold Tyler before she headed home.

They placed him on my chest, and the world hushed. No grandparents, no balloons, just us. Three became four, a family complete. For a few hours, we kept him ours. For a few hours, it felt like everything broken had been mended.

He was perfect. Warm, wide-eyed and serious. He reminded me of a little old man.

He was also very, very quiet.

Everyone said it like a blessing. "You're lucky he is such a quiet baby." I said it too because it seemed like the line I was supposed to deliver. But that first night I set an alarm every two hours not to feed a crying baby but to wake a silent one. Some part of me already knew: silence isn't always peace. Sometimes it's a warning you don't have the language for yet.

While Dad dozed on the stiff pullout and Jacob slept in a nest of blankets, I couldn't. The room was dark except for a slice of light under the door. Tyler lay beside me, warm and impossibly quiet. I pulled a scrap of notepaper from my bag and wrote a letter I'd never send.

The Letter

Dear Nanny,

You always know what to do. I'm sitting here with two boys, and I'm scared. How do you love two without splitting yourself in half? How do you stay strong enough when the world keeps taking the things you planned?

I can already picture them: Jacob teaching Tyler about trucks and dinosaurs. I hear whispers of made-up languages under blankets. They have muddy knees and matching haircuts. I want them to be brothers the way that saves you. I want to be strong enough to make that possible.

You're 3,300 miles away. If you were here, you'd shake your head and say I already know how: love them, keep going, don't quit. Just be strong like I was raised to be.

I will fail and keep going. One child will be loud and need the world; the other will be quiet and need a bridge. Help me be both anchor and oar. Tonight, I can hold three things true: Jacob's breath against the blanket, this baby's steady thrum under my palm, and the stubborn love you taught me.

If I do it wrong, I'll try again. If I break, I'll break quietly and then I'll make dinner. If they fall, I'll be the floor.

Silence

I folded the note and tucked it away like a talisman.
I told myself the quiet was a blessing after Jacob's colic.

I didn't know yet how much silence could mean.

The Baby Who Didn't Cry

Silence

Tyler didn't cry. Not when he was hungry. Not when he was cold. Not out of exhaustion… Not even when I left him too long, so I could tackle the growing mountain of laundry. Everyone called it a blessing. "Such an easy baby," they cooed. Lucky, they said. I didn't feel lucky. Babies are supposed to announce themselves: cry, cling, demand. Even curled against my chest, he felt far away, as if a pane of glass lived between us. He could go for hours without a sound. To anyone else, he was calm. To me, the quiet felt wrong.

Help

When Tyler was a few days old, Nana came to help. For a day or two, she did it all, rocked him so I could shower, loved Jacob, and kept the kitchen busy. Then her husband flew in, and sightseeing won. She deserves her fun; I was just desperate.

One night she offered to feed Tyler so I could take a long shower. I leapt. Minutes later she panicked… crashing into the shower like the world was on fire around us; she'd given him Jacob's whole milk instead of formula. He lay there, silent, no fuss, no cry, just… still. I thought he was a champ. Now I know it wasn't toughness. It was silence swallowing discomfort.

A day later, Dad, Nana, and Jacob ran to McDonald's in our beat-up '94 Escort, you know the kind you prayed over before turning the key. Cali traffic was just as bad then as it was now; somewhere along the line, Dad "cut someone off." An angry driver honked, raced, gestured, and eventually hurled a soda through their open window, drenching everyone and all but drowning my Big Mac. Nana shrieked,

Jacob wailed, and Dad white-knuckled the wheel. By the time they tumbled back in, fear had burned off, and the story was ridiculous. We laughed until our sides ached, sticky seats, soggy burger, one more chapter in young parenthood.

Tyler didn't flinch. Didn't turn toward the noise. Didn't track Nana's very loud voice. He lay in his basket, wide-eyed and untouched, as if he lived on a different frequency.

Alarms

My milk came in, then began to dry; my body betrayed me with lightning-bolt pain. I'd wake aching, arms too sore to lift, breasts burning, milk with nowhere to go. I'd reach into the bassinet and find Tyler wide awake and very hungry. I probably should have nursed; maybe everything would have been different. We had decided early on to use formula since Jacob nursed for almost two years. He refused bottles and pacifiers, so I was it for 20 months.

I didn't know Tyler would be so silent.

He never cried to wake me; pain did. I fed him in the dark, clumsy with bottles I'd only ever used on my siblings when I was thirteen. Some parts of me knew babies were supposed to demand. Another part made excuses: maybe this is how bottle babies are.

So, I set alarms for two, four, and six a.m. because silence wouldn't wake me. Jacob, barely two, padded in, climbed onto the couch, and helped tip the bottle with sticky hands. "Drink, baby, drink," he whispered, a toddler nurse on night shift. We were a team before we meant to be me terrified, Jacob steady, Tyler quiet.

There were no apps then, no monitors. Just SIDS pamphlets that contradicted each other and fear that didn't sleep. Doctors argued stomach versus back, wedges or no wedges, but none of them sat in the dark counting a silent baby's breaths.

Most nights I hovered until my back ached. When I couldn't see his chest rise, I touched his nose for the faintest brush of air. Sometimes I poked him just to be sure. Relief was the only thing louder than my heartbeat.

Home

Just before Tyler was born, we gave up hope of base housing and settled for a cheaper place forty-five minutes away. One bedroom near the border, thin walls, rattling pipes, neighbors who argued at midnight. The "master" fit one mattress on the floor, Dad's. The kids and I took the living room.

Dad worked bone-tired hours and snored like a freight train, so Jacob and I slept on an air mattress beneath the hum of the only TV we owned. Tyler's Moses basket sat beside us. The AC rattled like it was clinging to life; the place smelled like dust, formula, and the metallic tang of old heat.

We tried to make it home anyway. Jacob and I watched Lassie until his eyelids drooped. When we ran out of episodes, we put in his scratched Little Rascals DVD, "Little Bastards," he called it, and the name stuck. Tyler stilled at those voices, a tiny half-smile flickering at the edge of a silent face.

We had very little: a curbside couch, a borrowed table, and a rattling window. Yet, we enjoyed sweet nights together. Jacob giggled at Lassie while I stroked his hair. Tyler sat quietly, alert. In those moments, we created a feeling of safety.

The plan was to save. Housing allowance would cover rent; if we lived lean, we could build a cushion for the future. But formulas, special soaps, and new bottles ate every spare dollar. Still, there was laughter. Peanut-butter crackers on the floor. Movie nights on the air mattress. A toddler who believed he was my equal partner in raising his brother.

At night I did math on a legal pad: rent, gas, diapers, formula, soap (unscented), maybe one bargain-bin DVD if Jacob had a hard week. I wrote numbers like a spell that could conjure more. Sometimes we found quarters in the couch; sometimes we sold cans; sometimes the only thing left to cut was me.

Love isn't expensive until you're standing in a checkout line with a twenty disappearing into a tiny tub of hypoallergenic cream. I resented it for ten seconds, then rubbed it into Tyler's skin like penance. When he relaxed under my hands, I forgave the receipt.

Day

A typical day smelled like instant coffee and baby formula. Morning started before dawn; cheap coffee in a chipped mug; Jacob dragging his blanket; Tyler watching the ceiling fan spin. Coffee wasn't a drink so much as a lifeline.

No cell phones. No internet. A beige landline that tangled if you looked at it wrong. Email meant driving to the library. The world felt small, disconnected, and oddly quiet, like we were raising babies off the grid without meaning to.

Jacob built racetracks from couch cushions while I experimented with bottles and laundry soap that wouldn't rash Tyler's skin. Afternoons were cartoons and survival meals: peanut butter, canned soup, whatever stretched. Dad came home emptied out: boots heavy, lunch pail scraped clean. We squeezed around the tiny table and pretended the world wasn't as precarious as it felt. We found happiness and richness in these moments.

Bedtime was a ritual: a quick warm bath with the water turned off before Tyler came in (he hated the splash), Jacob giggling as he helped towel him dry, then the bright red Elmo snuggly that calmed him instantly. Bottle. Squeaky swing. Jacob leaning close to narrate the day.

My toddler invented the only rhythm that soothed his silent baby brother.

That rhythm saved me, too. I was twenty-one and scared. I felt exhausted. But those small, familiar routines (bath, Elmo, bottle, swing) brought structure to my days. Without them, it felt like I was falling.

Apnea

Three months in (just when I'd begun sleeping for more than two hours), the bottom dropped out.

The apartment was heavy with quiet. Jacob inches away on the air mattress. Tyler beside us in his basket. I woke up to a feeling, not a sound but that maternal intuition, the kind that yanks you upright before your brain catches up. I leaned over and touched him.

Cold.

Still.

For one heartbeat I couldn't find breath or pulse. My mind went white-hot and blank. Every cell screamed MOVE. I scooped him up, shaking, patting, rubbing, begging: "Breathe, baby, please breathe." The room tilted. My ears roared. "No, no, no," until the words broke and something inside me tore.

Then, with a tiny shudder, he inhaled. Color crept back into his lips. Air whooshed out of me in a ragged sob. Relief and horror braided together.

I didn't sleep again that night. Or many nights after. Fear moved in and sat at the edge of the air mattress. I carried him from room to room, unwilling to put more than a few feet between us. Rest felt like a risk I couldn't afford. If silence could steal him once, it could try again. The on-call doctor called it an apnea-like episode and wrote it off, saying isolated incidents do not warrant diagnosis or such panic, and to monitor him. So began the night shift.

Night Watch

I became a lighthouse. Every two hours, the beam of tiny light swept the room: air mattress, basket, and the small lift of ribs. I learned the apartment's language, the AC's death rattle, the neighbor's late news, the old fridge's hum. Any new sound lit me like a match.

I kept a hand mirror to fog under his nose when my eyes lied. A cool washcloth for the clamp around my chest. A quiet weather report for Jacob: we're okay, we're okay, we're okay. Most nights we were. Some nights the stillness made time double back. Those nights I counted to ten and touched Tyler's foot with one finger, bargaining with a God who was probably sleeping better than I was.

Errand

Our first grocery run felt like a test. Jacob rode in the cart, solemn as a captain; Tyler slept in the car seat clipped on top, hands folded like a saint. In the cereal aisle, an older woman touched my arm. "What a blessing," she said, eyes on Tyler. "An angel baby."

I smiled like I'd been handed a counterfeit bill. At checkout, a jar slipped from Jacob's hands and shattered. He cried. Tyler didn't blink. "You're lucky this one's so chill," the cashier said. I nodded and swallowed the urge to say, he's not chill, he's far away." In the parking lot sun, I buckled everyone in with shaking hands. Loneliness has a way of growing in crowded places.

Feeding

Feeding was a war. We spent money we didn't have chasing bottles and nipples. Every week, a new experiment with a new promise. Most landed in the trash.

One night, four bottles lined the counter, each with a different nipple. I rotated through them like a frantic game show. Formula dotted the floor. Tyler arched and refused, silent but fierce. When he finally drank, I was crying harder than he ever had.

I labeled nipples with a Sharpie like a lab tech: 1A, 1B, 2A, 2B, and took notes on flow, bubbles, and the way his tongue pushed or didn't. A neighbor swore by a European bottle you could only get by mail; I sent cash and a stamped envelope like contraband. It didn't work.

At three a.m. I'd hold a bottle sideways and watch a single drop creep toward the tip as if willing could turn it into what he needed. I learned the angle his chin wanted, the exact temperature his mouth would accept (not warm, not room—his). Victories were tiny and expensive. We paid in dollars, hours, and a sink full of failed plastic. If this were today's world, I would have taken him to the chiropractor for an adjustment to help his digestive system and regulate his overstimulated nervous system, but this was twenty years ago, and those things were not known.

Solids were worse. Purees made him gag. I cycled through peas, carrots, and applesauce like a desperate contestant. He clenched his lips, shuddered, and looked betrayed. I blamed the flavor. It was texture. Jacob tried to help, sneaking him a peanut like treasure. (Thank God Tyler ignored it; we would learn later how dangerous that gift could have been.)

Tags

Laundry day turned the apartment into a maze of drying lines. I ran each tag between my fingers, guessing which would be the enemy this week. Jacob and I would throw the laundry and Tyler into the hamper and together haul it down the steep stairs to the complex's laundry area. The dryer's thrum soothed Jacob: it wound Tyler tight. I cut out tags and left small ghosts of thread; sometimes the cut edge bothered him more.

I warmed blankets in the oven before swaddling. I scrubbed the tub with unscented soap until my knuckles split, then rinsed twice for the idea of fragrance. It felt ridiculous and holy at once, this priesthood of small accommodations, like love, could be proven by the absence of an itch.

Skin

It wasn't just tags. The wrong blanket. The brush of a sleeve. Bathwater at the wrong pitch. A hand too warm on his arm. The world overwhelmed him. Yet the red Elmo costume calmed him instantly. As if all his senses were turned past what the world should require.

I kept notes, soaps he tolerated, fabrics that didn't leave marks, temperatures that didn't make him flail. I charted what worked like a scientist in a small lab. Even with all that, doctors didn't listen. They patted my hand. "He'll grow out of it." Thus began the binder. It started as scrap notes in a folder and evolved over time. I would have traded this for another colicky baby any time. It was the price we paid for silence. A silence we didn't want or understand yet.

Dismissed

I tried to tell the doctors.

"He doesn't answer to his name."

"He doesn't play; he just stares or lines things up."

"He only wears one kind of outfit. Baths are a battle."

They smiled too brightly. "Boys take their time." "He'll be an engineer." "Einstein didn't talk until four."

Sugar over something bitter.

In the clinic, a fish tank big enough to make you forget you were paying to be ignored. Jacob named the plastic castle and counted blue rocks. Tyler watched the fluorescent light.

The paper on the exam table crackled like a dare. I listed concerns in a careful voice; the one women use when we've learned that panic is heard as nonsense. "He doesn't cry when he's hungry. He doesn't look when I call his name."

The doctor smiled at the chart, not us. "He's gaining," he said, as if that were the only song babies needed to sing. "Some kids are easy. Enjoy it." The house will be loud before you know it. He saw a girl too young to be a mother who just didn't understand the world. I vowed to prove him wrong.

On the drive home, I rehearsed the words I should have used: I don't need easy; I need to be present. I said nothing. The landline bill was due, and dinner wasn't going to make itself.

So I got educated. If knowledge were currency, I'd never be poor again. Parenting books stacked on the couch. Highlighters. Notebooks full of terms I barely understood. If that's what it took to be heard, I'd drown in research until they couldn't dismiss me.

Brother

Jacob was more than a toddler; he was our lifeline.

He toddled into the dark with me for every alarm, steadying the bottle while I fought sleep. He crawled beside Tyler's swing and narrated worlds: dinosaurs, trucks, peanut-butter crackers. He pressed toys into Tyler's hands like treaties. He was the only one who could coax him to pause, to focus, to connect.

Bedtime was his invention. He filled the gap when I was too tired to plan. He fetched the towel, turned off the bath water before Tyler came in, and helped slip him into the red Elmo snuggly. He patted the bottle against Tyler's lips and curled up beside the swing. "Night-night, baby," he whispered, rubbing a tiny forehead while I half-slept.

One afternoon I dozed on the couch while Jacob colored. I woke to his small voice describing every crayon line to his brother. And then it happened: Tyler smiled. His first real smile. Not for me. Not for Dad. For Jacob.

Jacob ran to me, chest puffed. "Mama! He likes me! He really likes me!"

Maybe part of me ached that it wasn't me. Mostly, I was grateful. My firstborn (barely out of toddlerhood) had crossed the invisible line between Tyler and the rest of us. Jacob wasn't just another child to care for; he was Tyler's first friend, first safe person, and first translator.

He was mine, too, an anchor on nights that felt endless. When I was sure I was failing, Jacob's calm told me we weren't entirely lost.

Again

Six weeks postpartum, still bone-tired and bleeding, I went to my checkup. The doctor came back smiling in a way that made my stomach drop. Pregnant. Again.

I asked for the test stick, slid it into my bag, and drove home in silence.

That afternoon I picked Dad up from work. Two exhausted little boys rattled in the back of our '94 Escort. I hadn't unbuckled them when I decided to rip the Band-Aid off. I handed him a small gift bag with the test inside.

He stared. "Are you kidding me? Really? Are you freaking kidding me?" He stepped away to the edge of the lot, hands on his head, silent.

I sat there in the driver's seat, milk-stained shirt, still healing, two babies behind me, and felt the ground tilt. He would come around. He always did. But at that moment, I had never felt more alone.

The next day he slid into the passenger seat with a paper sack of cinnamon twists, as if sugar could apologize. "I was shocked," he said, eyes forward. "I'm sorry." I nodded. Sorry was real and not enough. Maybe the shock came from the one moment we had together in the last two months; maybe it was the thought of three when two was such an adjustment, but shock was there just the same.

That night he put Jacob to bed and came back smelling like bubble bath and baby shampoo, the tenderness he has for his boys softening the sharp angles the Corps builds. He rested a cautious hand on my belly, like the test might change its mind if he pressed too hard. "We'll figure it out," he said. We usually did. Figuring it out isn't the same as being okay, but it's a start.

Strangers would later argue with me in aisles…two babies the same size. "Twins?" they'd ask. I'd shake my head. Ten months apart. Irish twins. It sounded like a joke God tells when He's bored.

Back then, it was just two car seats and a world that required four hands I didn't have. Jacob puffed up anyway. "I help," he said, and he did. He would be the bridge I didn't know we needed.

This time I wasn't scared of losing a baby. I feared keeping him, of keeping all of us afloat. Some part of me already knew my instinct about Tyler wasn't wrong, and that life was about to get harder.

Reflection

I told myself silence was peace, that maybe I had been given a quiet baby, an easy baby, when Jacob was full of colic and noise. But the quiet lingered, both heavy and strange, filling every room like a fog. By the time I realized something was missing, he was already gone. Then the house felt even more silent. The world would keep shifting under my feet, from desert dust to highway miles, and I told myself it was just another move, another apartment, another start.

He's Not Even Here

The bed was still warm when I rolled over, but he wasn't there. He had left like he always did, uniform pressed, bag at the door, duty, honor, and country first. This time, though, he was not coming home in a few days. The house still smelled like coffee and aftershave, and for a moment, I could pretend he was just late. But he wasn't he was gone.

Deployment

By August, the Texas heat had settled in like a punishment. The baby fat on Tyler's legs glistened with sweat before breakfast, and the box fan in our Mesquite apartment never stopped humming. We'd traded the border town for something closer to family (his idea). He said it would be easier on me once he shipped out. I nodded, pretending that proximity to his family could fill the silence he was leaving behind.

Dad deployed. Tyler didn't notice.

War was supposed to look like uniforms, salutes, and flags snapping in the wind. In our house, it looked like silence.

The goodbye scene at the airport was almost scripted, like something out of a military commercial. My Marine in pressed uniform, our family clutching juice cups and the stroller, red-white-and-blue banners held high in an attempt to feel like we were part of the cause. There were camera flashes, little American flags waving, tears caught in glossy photographs. Hugs like they were made to be in a movie; dramatic, tearful, perfectly timed. But to me, it all felt hollow, as if I were standing on the set of a play I didn't audition for.

Jacob clung to my leg, confused but quiet, his big eyes darting from Dad to the strangers we told him were our family, and Tyler sat in his stroller, spinning the buckle over and over in his hands. The terminal echoed with voices, footsteps, and squeaking wheels, but Tyler's world was reduced to that piece of plastic in his lap. He didn't cry when Dad knelt in front of him. He didn't look up. He didn't even pause.

I wanted to scream, to beg for just one moment of connection between father and son. For Tyler to notice. For him to reach out. But Dad kissed his forehead anyway, smiling through exhaustion, pretending not to notice the absence. Then he scooped Jacob into his arms, pressing his face into our toddler's hair. "Take care of Mommy," he whispered.

And then it was my turn.

He smelled like stress and starch, like long hours and tension stitched into fabric. His hug was quick, his kiss hurried, because duty waited for no one. Then he turned, merged into the crowd, and just like that, he was gone.

The Home Front

The patriotic posters promised pride and honor, but the drive home was nothing but silence. Two kids in the backseat. One unborn baby shifting inside me. My hands gripping the steering wheel so tightly the skin on my knuckles stretched white. I stared through the windshield, but my chest was heavy with the weight of everything coming.

The military told us deployments were about honor and sacrifice, about bravery and service. But they didn't talk about the wives driving home from airports with toddlers in the back seat and contractions already threatening to start. They didn't talk about the quiet houses where uniforms hung in closets like ghosts while pregnant women tried to breathe through panic alone. They promised the return of our soldiers in six months with no warning of how easily it could turn into thirteen.

I told myself I'd be fine. Women did this all the time, didn't they? I would manage the nights alone, the mornings with cereal spilled on the counter, the appointments, the meltdowns, the swollen belly pressing against me. I rehearsed strength as if it were a script. But deep down, I knew I was unprepared.

Labor

Dad had only been gone a few weeks when the labor started. They would inject me to stop it for only two weeks. These two weeks had broken me down, contractions that came in waves then were stopped with a quick shot just when I thought I couldn't take another breath. Each time I was sent home from the hospital, I was still pregnant, still waiting, still bracing.

So, when it finally started again, I decided to continue my day as normal. I went to the market with Nana, telling her each grimace was just gas; I ate my dinner with a smile. There would be no calm announcement, no hospital bag by the door, no husband's steady hand on my back. Just me, two children, and pain so sharp it took my voice.

That night, it got worse. At first, just an ache, the familiar cramping I had learned to dismiss after two long weeks of starting and stopping. I told myself it was nothing I couldn't handle, that I could push through it the way I always did.

The contractions gripped hard, sharp enough to make me double over. I tried a hot shower, steam curling around me, hoping the water would ease the pain. It didn't. My voice trembled as I called my sister, pretending I was calm, my words clipped between waves of pain. She tried to reassure me, but even I could hear the fear in her voice. She couldn't distract me from the pain this time.

Jacob curled beside me on the bed; his warm little body pressed against my belly as if he could protect me from the pain. He was always my snuggle bug, my shadow, my steady little soul. He rubbed my stomach with his small hand, whispering in his sing-song voice, "It's okay, Mommy. I'll help." The pain intensified, so I moved us all to the living room and lay on the floor. It was about this time he scrambled for his precious baseball mitt that had once belonged to his dad, slipped it on proudly, and announced, "I'll catch the baby when it comes out of your butt!" His eyes were so wide, so serious, that I almost laughed through the tears.

Tyler, meanwhile, sat across the room, eyes fixed on the glow of Dumbo or "Jumbo," as Jacob always called it. He didn't look over. Didn't flinch at my cries. Didn't notice Jacob bouncing on my belly like a tiny midwife. Instead, he ripped my Friends DVDs from the shelf, one by one, chewing on the cardboard covers like they were teething toys.

I ached for him to crawl into my arms, to want me, to need me. But he stayed in his own current, detached from the chaos, untouched by my pain. And the thought I hated most slid into my mind again, sharp and cruel: Tyler doesn't like me. It was something I thought daily and vocalized many times.

The contractions came faster. My legs buckled under me. My breathing turned to ragged gasps. I called my mother-in-law at last, my voice cracking with panic as I tried to form words through agony. Jacob clutched my phone in his little hands, passing it to me when I needed it, then rubbing my back when I cried out. He never left my side. She asked one too many times if I was sure it was the real deal before I snapped, "YES, GET YOUR ASS HERE QUICK.

When Nana finally burst through the door, her panic filled the house. She had been unable to wake Dad's sister, so she would just have to meet us there. She scooped Jacob into her arms, grabbed Tyler by the hand, and wrapped her arm around me as I clung to the wall, every muscle seizing. The cold night air hit my face as we stumbled outside. Her voice shook as she promised it would be okay, though we both knew we were running out of time.

We sped toward the hospital, the car lurching around corners as contractions ripped through me. My body was in full labor. My mind was numb. Nana ran red lights, defied driving odds, and at one moment I think she had the car airborne. All the while telling me, don't you push, you better not have that baby in this car.

We arrived at the hospital to meet a refusal to help me in. Against hospital policy (I wonder how many babies are born in that parking lot), a nurse on some break saw the struggle to get out and take a step and rushed us into the delivery ward. They threw me in a gown and lifted me onto the bed in a blur of chaos. A doctor rushed in, shoving his hand in me without even a hello. Then, in all his wisdom, he determined the baby was not engaged; therefore, he could not be born and promptly left. Deciding I was not yet worth his time. Like most Tricare-approved doctors I had experienced, he refused to listen when I said my babies don't engage; they just come. A fact that would hold true for all 7 deliveries.

And then, moments later, Thomas was born, so fast the doctor didn't even make it back into the room. No epidural. No husband's hand to squeeze. No calm or control. Just me, my aunt, and sister-in-law, as I was split open in fluorescent light, delivering a baby into a world that already felt both full and hollow at the same time. He was caught by my aunt, and quickly, medical personnel rushed in.

The next little bit was a blur of NICU visits, chaos, and surviving on soda and candy bars. A well-intentioned nurse made a mistake, and Thomas spent a week in the NICU instead of a few hours.

And Tyler? A week later, when I brought Thomas home wrapped in blankets, Tyler didn't even notice. My body had broken, my arms cradled a newborn, our family had shifted forever. But in Tyler's world, nothing had changed.

Home with Baby

The first week home with Thomas felt less like recovery and more like survival training. There was no gentle postpartum glow, no quiet days of healing with casseroles dropped at the door. My body was still raw, stitched, and aching, but the world didn't pause to let me recover.

Bottles piled in the sink until they smelled sour. Burp rags stiffened in laundry baskets. Diapers stacked like sandbags waiting for the next wave. I kept Thomas strapped to my chest in a sling so I could move with both hands free, my body a makeshift base camp, always ready. I nursed him while giving Tyler his bottle, and he slept soundly against me while I folded clothes, made calls, or tried to keep Tyler safe.

Tyler moved through the house like a shadow, unaffected by the screaming infant against my chest. He didn't recoil, but he didn't reach for him either. He lined up his toys with quiet precision, the hum of Dumbo in the background, his world untouched by the new cries filling mine.

Jacob, though, Jacob noticed everything. At four years old, he was my right hand, my shadow, my little soldier. He fetched diapers with solemn focus, patted Thomas's back when I fixed Tyler's lunch, and brought me a glass of water when I forgot to drink for hours. His eyes scanned me constantly, reading me in ways no child should have had to.

Sometimes, I'd find proof of just how much he carried in the smallest details. After pumping milk, I'd rush to the shower, leaving the bags on the counter, meaning to put them away later. More than once, I'd come back to find them already tucked neatly in the fridge.

Jacob, at only three, barely tall enough to see the counter, had climbed onto a chair, organized the milk carefully, and lined it up with the precision of a grown man. No one taught him. He just saw what needed to be done.

It broke my heart and mended it all at once. He was a child carrying the weight of two worlds: his own and mine. His quiet, steady love melted me more than words ever could. I would spend my lifetime trying to repay him for all he did.

Nights were the hardest. Exhaustion pressed down like smoke, wrapping around me until I couldn't tell one day from the next. I'd rock Thomas in the dark, Jacob asleep curled in his small bed, Tyler humming from across the hall, detached but steady. And I'd wonder if this was what war really felt like: not bombs and bullets, but days that blurred into each other until you forgot what month it was, nights when silence felt heavier than gunfire, mornings when you wondered if you had the strength to rise again.

Parallel War

Dad went to war overseas.

I went to war in my living room.

Sometimes, Dad would call. The connection was always bad; his voice crackled with static, and background noise swallowed his words. I'd smile into the phone, forcing a cheerful tone while cradling a fussy newborn and watching Tyler line up toys on the floor.

"We're fine," I'd say brightly, stepping over laundry piles, wiping spit-up from my shirt with one hand. "Everyone's good."

Tyler didn't look up. He never reacted to the sound of his dad's voice through the speaker.

I'd hang up and cry quietly in the kitchen, hating myself for making things sound easier than they were. But what was I supposed to say? That I was drowning? That I didn't even know if Tyler would notice if his dad came home tomorrow? That this wasn't the kind of "strong military wife" anyone wanted to put on a poster? The only preparation you get as a spouse before deployment is the stern talk telling you not to give them bad news, not to distract them from the mission, and to make sure the soldier feels like the world is right as rain no matter the truth.

The Small Battles

Deployment meant constant small battles. The car broke down once, and I sat at the stoplight sobbing, staring at the smoke curling from the hood while the baby wailed and Tyler covered his ears. I made do with what I had: duct tape, borrowed rides, and prayer. There were days I couldn't even remember when I last ate.

Friends offered help, but no one could really understand. A neighbor once told me, "You're so strong. I don't know how you do it." I smiled and said thank you, but inside I wanted to scream. I wasn't strong; I was breaking every day.

And then there was Tyler. My beautiful, mysterious boy, so disconnected from the world that even war couldn't shake him. He didn't notice the empty boots by the door or the folded flags. He didn't ask where Dad was or why I cried at night. His world stayed steady while mine spun out of control.

First

"Fuck. Fuck. Fuck."

Those were Tyler's first spontaneous words.

Not Mama. Not Dada. Just fuck.

We were in the slightly beat-up Ford Taurus we kept alive with duct tape, Band-Aids, oil we couldn't afford, and stubbornness, headed to Paw Paw's on a Texas afternoon that stuck to your skin. Vinyl seats were hot, AC wheezing, car smelling like stale Cheerios and car seat milk.

Jacob was strapped in, "helping" baby Thomas with his bottle and angling for sips of my warm soda. We passed snacks across seats, half-sang a rap song through static, and for one fragile minute it felt like we were getting away with it, joy despite the math of our lives.

A duck waddled out like it had a death wish.

I jerked the wheel. "FUCK!"

Silence. Then a small, perfect echo from the car seat: "Fuck."

Again, delighted: "Fuck. Fuck."

Crisp. Cheerful. Like he'd stored the word in a secret pocket waiting for his cue. Jacob exploded into belly laughs. The harder he laughed, the brighter Tyler got, tiny fists bouncing, chanting like a drummer who found the beat. I bribed them with everything I could think of just to get them to hush. By Paw Paw's driveway, my cheeks burned with embarrassment and my chest ached with something I hadn't held in too long: hope.

Inside, Tyler paraded his new trick. "Duck," I lied. Nobody believed me. I didn't either. But if sound could break through once, maybe silence wasn't welded shut.

Dad wasn't there to hear the beautiful and grown-up word repeatedly rush out of Tyler. It was me, a Taurus with a prayer, and three little lifetimes buckled in the back. I clung to that single word like a rope. Later I would learn what echolalia was, but in this moment it was a spontaneous word, a glimmer of hope.

Then came the quiet.

Dad missed so much when Tyler was born. Deployment math ignores due dates. There's a vacuum to that kind of absence. You learn to carry it while you carry car seats.

Invisible War

Nights were the worst.

There were nights I'd stand over Thomas's bassinet, Tyler asleep in his bed, Jacob curled up in his bed, and I'd just… stand there. Watching their tiny chests rise and fall, my own exhaustion was heavier than my body could bear.

Some nights, I'd lie on the floor beside Tyler's bed. Sometimes I'd put my hand near him, not touching, just close enough to feel his warmth. We'd lie there back-to-back, awake, breathing the same air, carrying two different wars.

That year I learned how invisible love can feel. How heavy silence can be. How far away someone can drift even when they're sitting right next to you.

I prayed, not for deployments to end, not for duty to ease, but for a crack in the silence. For Tyler to see me. For him to see anyone.

Because sometimes the hardest part wasn't when Dad was gone. It was that even when he came back, Tyler didn't.

Somewhere inside me, I had believed Dad's return would be a reset button. That the duffle bag dropped on the floor, the boots by the door, the embrace in the entryway would somehow stitch us back together. That Tyler would notice. That he'd run to his father, smile, laugh, or give us one of those hugs that melt a parent into their child.

The Homecoming

But when Dad walked back through the door a year later, Tyler didn't move. He didn't run. He didn't even look up. The duffle bag thudded to the floor, the house filled with uniforms and relief, but Tyler's world stayed steady, untouched.

I stood there in the doorway, ten-month-old on my hip, Jacob tugging at my sleeve, and Tyler humming to himself, lost in a rhythm I couldn't reach. Dad had come home, but Tyler hadn't.

And that was the hardest truth of all. The military painted sacrifice in red, white, and blue. But my sacrifice was invisible. It was a child who felt oceans away even when he was sitting three feet from me.

He wasn't gone. He was right there in front of me.

But he wasn't here either.

Not really.

And I realized then that the war I was fighting wasn't about deployments or homecomings. It was about finding a way to reach my son in a world where he didn't even seem to see me. When I thought we had finally settled, it was time to re-enlist another duty station on the map and another move for our family. Beaufort, South Carolina, here we come. The move was made easier with the hope that maybe here I would find someone to understand and listen to what I saw in Tyler. To what instinct told me was not typical.

Restarting

I didn't know yet how much silence could mean. But I was about to learn how quickly it can leave and how fast it can return.

Fade

Regression doesn't kick your door in. It loosens hinges until one day lunch is burning and the door is just… gone.

Months passed since we arrived in Beaufort, South Carolina. The sun-battered base housing stood firm. Stubborn grass grew everywhere under a sky that screamed as jets tore through it. The air after rain tasted mineral and green. Sand-fine soil sifted between our toes.

We dragged trikes out. Jacob launched a football to nobody and chased it himself. I handed out box-mix cupcakes with frosting and sprinkles I pretended made up for everything else. I set Tyler on the porch by the window so I could watch him; he sat, cupcake in hand, observing like we were a TV show he didn't mind but wouldn't join.

I grabbed the digital camera. Back then I took fifty photos a day like proof could trap time. "Tyler, smile," I called. He didn't. He didn't even glance up when the shutter clicked. Someone once told me the things we photograph most are the things we are afraid to lose. Overtime that has held true for me, but back then it hit me hard. I did not want to lose these innocent days. The days when summer playing and box-mix cupcakes could heal all wounds.

That night, after cadence calls faded and a jet gnawed the horizon, I loaded the photos onto our wheezing desktop. Jacob: feral grin, frosting everywhere. Thomas: gummy smile, eyes like bright pennies. Tyler: pond-still. No spark. Not even the polite camera smile he used to give on command. When edited black and white, it reminded me of one of those commercials set to sad music to try to elicit donations.

My breath caught before my brain found the words.

The next day he wouldn't throw the ball to Jacob. He picked up a plastic golf club and tapped careful arcs near us, rarely with us.

Fan

Another base house that smiled wrong. The kids swore it was haunted. One bedroom stayed empty; even Jacob wouldn't cross the threshold. "A little boy lives in the mirror," he whispered, "and he doesn't want us here; he just wants you to be his mommy." Ghosts or gut, kids know when a house holds its breath. That hallway stayed cold. Floorboards sighed without feet. The closet mirror seemed to have its own weather.

I laughed it off for them. Alone, I watched that mirror too long.

Pregnant again, number four, exhaustion lived behind my eyes. One night we half-watched Wizards of Waverly Place with Jacob while Thomas snoozed beside us. Tyler played alone in his room, content in a rhythm only he could hear.

The sound didn't just happen; it arrived. A crack like thunder widened a seam. The hall filled with drywall dust. The ceiling fan lay on the carpet in pieces, blades splayed like shrapnel, motor housing dented. Tyler sat beneath it, blood webbing his hairline, eyes wide and nowhere.

Everything narrowed: towel, pressure, prayer without words. Dad called for an ambulance while I clung to my young child. ER lights fluoresced hard enough to ache. Antiseptic bit my nose. A nurse asked questions as if information could hold the world up. Tyler sat stiff, shock swallowing him whole. When the needle touched skin, he didn't cry. He didn't flinch. He said one thing, flat and looping, as if the words were the only solid ground: "Bam. Tyler boo-boo."

He said it the next day, and the next, standing in the doorway like a guard at his own memory. Joy slipped through him like water. Trauma stuck like glue.

Later, curiosity won. I searched through old base records, a newspaper clipping: a little boy had died in that room during a fire. The fan that hit Tyler was part of the hasty repairs. Suddenly, every creak felt loaded. Maybe the house wasn't haunted. It sure as hell wasn't safe. Less than a year after we moved, those units were condemned for asbestos and leaking fuel tanks. We were just one more young family shoved inside. We would be the last family to spend an enlistment there. The last babies brought into the poisoned and possibly haunted home.

Day

A day in that season smelled like reheated coffee and baby wipes.

Mornings began before they deserved to. Cheap coffee in a chipped mug, reheated twice, was what I called breakfast.

The light was that Dad was home more. This duty station allowed a little more time for family.

Jacob ran point like a four-year-old foreman, "reading" the list he couldn't read, lining socks by color, perfecting the routine he invented when I ran out of invention. We did not live by clocks or schedules, just routine.

Afternoons, the boys fought over trikes while I researched two-year-olds with no words, light sensitivity, and texture aversion. So many things that still didn't have a name. Evenings, Dad or no Dad, we circled the tiny table and pretended the world wasn't as thin as it was. Night was lamplight, printouts, cold coffee, and crumbs under bare feet, me telling the air: stay awake, keep fighting.

Some nights, after the folders closed, I wrote letters I never sent to Nanny, to my mom, or just to the void. I'd confess I was scared and failing and the boys needed more than a half-awake mother. If Nanny were there, she'd twist pretzels and tell me to keep going. I tucked the notes into the folders' pockets like prayers between pages. Slowly, my folders were evolving into the binder.

War

After the fan, the slope steepened. Eye contact evaporated. His name hung unanswered. Play collapsed into order: rows, spins, taps— the same moves in new rooms. Illness hid; he'd sleep in vomit rather than cry. Open-ended questions were landmines. "Tyler bam. Tyler boo-boo." That's how he told you a storm had passed through him.

Doctors smiled with their mouths, not their eyes.

"Boys develop more slowly."

"He'll be an engineer."

"You're overthinking."

In waiting rooms, the fish tanks bubbled like a joke. Why were there always fish tanks? Cartoon murals promised kindness that clipboards didn't deliver. I said, "He doesn't answer to his name," and the pediatrician patted my hand like a dog. I left carrying a preschooler, two toddlers, and rage sharp enough to cut glass. Even Dad, for a while, shrugged. "He's like you," he said. "Quirky. Needs order." " He is just going to be less emotion-driven and more systematic; he sees you do it." Maybe. Or maybe a tide was pulling our boy out while we called it a puddle.

Binder nights became a ritual. Lamp on, house asleep, me awake. The living room full of crumbs, laundry, sippy cups, crayons, a stroller wheel that kept popping free, turned into a war room. Library printouts bled highlighter. Timelines. Checklists. Sensory logs. Appointment notes where I was polite and not heard. I spread photos across the floor like tarot and read our life back: the moment light drained from his gaze; the hum I'd labeled sweet now "self-stimulation;" early right-hand dominance stamped RED FLAG in a journal I barely understood.

I wasn't chasing a cure. Tyler wasn't broken. I was hunting for a map. Hope became currency, and I hoarded it; any story of a kid who "caught up" was oxygen I rationed.

Guilt moved in with a suitcase.

Tyler was the only one I didn't nurse.

The only one whose vaccinations I didn't argue about the timing when a nurse even doubled a dose and looked more rattled than I did.

No, I don't believe vaccines alone cause autism. I do believe bodies keep score and the world tugs on threads genetics spun. Would nursing have changed his story? Maybe my milk would have given him something that formula couldn't. Waiting a bit on the vaccines? Pushing harder in a room of white coats? I'll never know. Guilt is a brick you carry even when your hands are full of babies.

Twins

We were still in survival after the fan, Tyler with a new scar; I with new insomnia, when I dared Target with all three. I loaded the boys into the squeaky double stroller; Jacob walked proudly, "in charge" of the list. Big-box air: popcorn, plastic, sugar.

Popcorn was our splurge. One salty tub. One soda with two straws. "Target fuel," I told Jacob, knighting him with the first handful. He glowed. Tyler went still at the rumble of the popcorn machine, eyes fixed but calm. For a few bites we weren't broke or overwhelmed; we were just four people savoring salt and survival.

Halfway down the baby aisle, a woman stopped us, all teeth. "Oh my gosh, you have twins?"

"Irish twins," I said. "Ten months apart."

She studied their faces like a math problem. Tyler slumped, gaze sliding past. Thomas babbled at the fluorescents like old friends. "Really?" she said. "They look the same age."

Something bristled. Maybe exhaustion. Maybe the new ache. I wanted to say, "One is quietly leaving, and I don't know how to follow. Instead, I smiled too tightly and kept rolling.

Jacob spun on his heel, hands on hips. "They're NOT twins," he announced. "Tyler's a little bigger. He's just…quiet."

Quiet hung heavier than it should. Quiet wasn't shy anymore. Quiet was the gulf I was learning to cross with a binder and a prayer.

We paid for our diapers, then tore into popcorn and split the soda at the little round table by the exit like kings. Jacob leaned against me, salt on his lips, happy. I held that one small, good thing like it could carry us. For as long as I could make my kids feel happy, I would be able to survive it all.

The Cupcake Point

I was frosting cupcakes. Justin slept in the bassinet. Jacob and Thomas argued over crayons. Tyler hovered.

He still wasn't talking much. Usually, a brother translated. This time, there was no interpreter. He looked at me. Really looked, eyes steady, and lifted one finger to point at the cooling cupcake.

No words. No manners. But it was intentional. Direct.

I set the cupcake in his hand and let silence be praise. The next day I moved the milk out of reach and waited. A glance, another point. On day three, a whisper "mm" and I celebrated like Shakespeare. Connection first. Language later. Everything about how I taught him changed.

The world kept asking when he'd catch up, as if different meant late. Tyler wasn't behind. He was on his own timeline—written in repetition, bravery, and do-overs. Showers, teeth, cupcakes—none of it charts cleanly, but its movement.

Every time Tyler points now—for food, for space, for understanding, I think of that cupcake. The simplicity of it. The quiet miracle of being seen. It would be so easy for the world to mistake that silence for absence; to miss the thousand small ways he reaches out every day. But I've learned to read him fluently: the lift of a finger, the hum that means contentment, the pause that means a question.

More

This season of our life was the loudest one. Jacob shared his stories as he began kindergarten. Thomas learned to talk. Tyler quietly spun wheels. Food was a battlefield; Jacob ate anything, Thomas only wanted nuggets, and Tyler, well, applesauce betrayed him. Pasta insulted him. He ate by ritual or not at all.

One afternoon he wanted a candy bar. Normally I'd hand it over for five minutes of peace. But instinct bridged to decision. I needed a word not for me, but for him. A first rung where his foot could land.

I held the chocolate just out of reach. "Say something," I asked. Eat. More. Chocolate. Any word.

Tyler screamed, reached, and turned to his translator.

Jacob, five and already the best man I knew, stepped in, palms up. "Mama, he wants it. I'll say it."

"I know, baby," I kept my voice even. "This time he has to try."

Jacob crouched to meet his eyes. "Tyler," he whispered like a coach, "say more. You can do it."

Tyler sobbed, grabbing past him. Jacob stayed steady, whispering the word like rope. Guilt hissed: Your child has enough going on and you're withholding chocolate? But motherhood isn't a likeability contest. It's the long game.

Tyler's eyes snapped to mine, wet, furious, and present. I would not give in, and somehow, he knew it.

"More," he said.

Lightning. I shoved chocolate into his hand. Another piece for another word. "More chocolate." I said questioningly. "More," Tyler said more confidently this time. Jacob whooped like we'd won the championship, clapping until his cheeks went pink. That night we ate Hershey's for dinner and laughed until we cried. When Dad got home, Jacob staged a reenactment. "Say it, Ty!" Tyler obliged. We cheered like the house was a stadium and the team finally scored.

Jacob took the coach role seriously. The living room became a speech boot camp disguised as play. Matchbox cars lined up; Jacob whispered names for Tyler to repeat: "red," "fast," "zoom." Picture books became scripts with wild gestures. Sometimes he lay beside Tyler on the carpet, chanting "more" until giggles turned to words.

When someone asked if he felt jealous, Jacob shook his head. "I taught him," he said, like a scientist who found fire.

Within a week, words poured in. Breakfast turned into a chorus of requests. Car rides turned into questions. Tyler pointed at birds and tried out their names. He sang along to commercials, stretching the vowels. He tested language like a new toy he just couldn't stop playing with. Therapists said "breakthrough." I didn't care which label stuck. My boy had a voice. And Jacob, who carried it for so long, never acted replaced. He was proud. Gloriously proud.

And once the sentences came, they didn't stop. Slowly at first, tentative echoes of things he heard us say. Therapists called it echolalia. Doctors called it scripting. I didn't care what they called it; I called it hope.

Because love doesn't always show up the way you expect it to. Sometimes it's loud and easy. Sometimes it's a whisper you wait years to hear. Sometimes it arrives after silence has buried you so deep you've stopped believing.

But when it comes, it shakes the ground.

Lessons

Regression felt like walking backward in the dark, terrifying, guilt-heavy, and lonely. But it wasn't final.

Tyler didn't stay lost. He didn't stay silent. He restarted.

I stopped chasing checklists and started chasing connection: a hum that answered my lullaby, a forehead pressed to mine in the quiet, a hard-won *more* that opened a door. Progress wasn't linear, but it was ours.

Every day I told myself: we aren't chasing milestones. We're chasing moments, a look, a laugh, a word cracked open like a window.

On the days the window slammed, we waited. Then we tried again.

Line in the Sand

Line in the Sand

It was Tyler and me against the world. I drew that line early because no one else seemed to understand.

There was a single moment that made me finally snap; years of moments just like it had preceded, but this day was the last day I would be told no when it came to services for my son. It would be the day I started to fight not only for him but for every special needs child being told no. It wasn't a grand speech or some insightful moment. It was a hallway outside a therapy office where a receptionist said there were no openings "for kids like him" until spring. I smiled, thanked her, walked out, and gathered my thoughts calmly from the parking lot. I went back in, and by the time I was in that hallway again, we had a Thursday cancellation appointment set up. The line wasn't loud. It was immovable.

Before that hallway, I used to believe that being polite was the same as being strong.

I thought if I said "please" and "thank you" enough times, the world would meet me halfway. I smiled through ignorance, nodded at advice I didn't ask for, and waited for understanding that never arrived. The world doesn't hand out grace to quiet mothers; it mistakes softness for weakness.

The first time someone dismissed me with a shrug, a nurse telling me "He'll grow out of it" while never looking up from the chart, I felt something in me harden. I went home shaking, wrote her name on a sticky note, and promised myself I'd never walk out of a room unheard again. But I did several times before I had become hardened enough and desperate enough to learn how to understand my son that I would never be quiet again. That was the real beginning of the line in the sand: not anger, but refusal. Refusal to disappear.

A lot of times we would get asked, "When does Tyler catch up?" At this stage in our journey when people asked, "When will he catch up?" I smiled and said, "When he's ready." Inside, I was screaming; outside, I was polite. As if development were a race and my child had simply forgotten to tie his shoes. As if it were a delay, not a different path.

The Fight for Answers

Back when bath time needed a rule sheet and Jacob's help, we finally got in to see a developmental neurologist and psychologist. One of the most sought-after names. Four hours away but well worth the drive. He was one of the best and a man we would grow to love because he heard us. The waitlist was brutal; the drive was long, but we got in.

In the clinic, another damn aquarium hummed. Forms blurred. During testing, they slid pattern blocks across the table. Tyler didn't look at the tester; he looked at the pieces the way some kids look at candy. "Match the picture," she said. He finished before her pen touched the paper. I tried not to gasp.

The doctor watched him in quiet awe for a minute, chin resting on one hand. "He's very visual," he murmured, eyes still on the blocks. "You notice that?"

I nodded, afraid to breathe wrong, afraid to look too proud.

"You're not imagining it," he said finally. "His brain is moving faster than he can get the words out. He's not ignoring you. He's busy."

This amazing man spent hours observing, questioning, and testing Tyler. Tyler thought he was just playing, but every puzzle he put together in under two minutes, every toy he ignored, and the ones he clung to told this Dr. something, and we finally started getting answers.

No one had ever said I wasn't imagining things before. For years, every worry had been smoothed over, every question waved away like a gnat. I wanted to hug this stranger in his sensible shoes. Instead, I nodded until my throat hurt, pressing my nails into my palm to keep from crying. Validation felt foreign, almost painful, sunlight in a room that had been dark for too long.

That night, driving home with Tyler asleep in the backseat, I replayed that sentence over and over: You're not imagining it. It became a mantra, proof that I wasn't crazy, that my gut was smarter than the noise. Sometimes a diagnosis isn't what saves you; it's the permission to trust yourself again.

A few days later, Dad and I would go back, and we would add another chapter to the binder. The chapter that gave everything a name. Something to begin to understand. A chapter that came with more questions than answers but also gave us something we could learn to understand: "Severe Infantile Autism Classic." This is what they called it back then; now he would be simply "ASD Level 3."

When he was first diagnosed, official estimates of autism had already begun climbing, and the myths were thick; most people assumed autism usually paired with intellectual disability. Tyler shattered that. His testing came back high, off the charts in certain areas. Visual-spatial tasks? Surgical. Rotating shapes in his head, solving designs upside down. Language? He stared at the floor and hummed. The graph looked like a skyline: one tower scraping clouds, the next barely a story high. "Asynchronous," they called it. I called it proof there was a city in there; lights on, elevators running, if only I could learn the streets.

They said even though he was not "intellectually disabled," he would probably always be non-verbal (non-speaking is the term of today). They said he would likely never toilet train because communication is a huge part of that. They even went so far as to say he would most likely end up institutionalized. Dad took this to heart. You could see the worry in his eyes, the stress of this label hitting him all at once. I decided in this moment that Tyler would be the one to make these doctors eat their words. I took this as a challenge that Tyler and I would take on together.

Awareness isn't the same as understanding. Mothers clung to the few experts who would see them. Each book promised hope or war, sometimes both. Some people chased cures. Some blamed shots, medication, or food. Mostly we clawed at each other for resources that didn't exist. If you weren't loud, your kid was invisible. In a way, maybe we all were right, but in this era of autism, we had little to go on, and a few of us were coming together to change the way for the generations ahead.

That was the season when I dug my heels into that line and refused to move.

Culture Then 2006 to 2013

Autism wasn't mainstream. No YouTube sensory hacks. No TikTok advocates. No picture charts waiting in every classroom. Chuck E. Cheese wasn't dimming lights for sensory mornings.

We had dirty looks, unsolicited advice, and silence.

When Tyler was four, a very ignorant leader looked at Dad and said, "Why don't you just throw a helmet on him?" The world saw something to pad, not a child to understand. I felt the heat rise. "He doesn't need armor," Dad said evenly. "He needs predictability." That night I wrote a letter: polite, documented, undeniable. The letter became a meeting. The meeting became a small change to a drill schedule. Not a revolution. A brick. Dad found anger in this moment; I found a way to change the perception.

Learning to Fight

My first real win wasn't glamorous. An email chain. I asked for a visual schedule in class. Silence. I asked again. I copied three people. I attached a research excerpt. I offered to make it myself. Then I showed up with laminated cards and Velcro.

The principal frowned. The teacher shrugged. Two weeks later, Tyler transitioned without melting down. I didn't gloat. I brought extra Velcro for the next kid.

This was when I got that question again… "When do you think he'll max out?" as if he were a battery with a percentage bar. What I wanted to say: Tyler doesn't max out. He restarts.

I vowed he would not be folded into anyone's grim statistics. If the system didn't bend, I would. I would rock the boat and keep rocking it until the water made space. Tyler didn't have a voice yet, so I learned to be loud for both of us. Years later, he would repay it tenfold—defying odds and forcing changes in a military system that didn't know what to do with kids like him.

Family Rules & Sibling Lessons

Life wasn't only meltdowns and shame. Between routines and scraped knees, Tyler surprised us. His siblings learned quickly that his silence could be useful. I'd find a kitchen mess or pee in the Lego bin and hear, "Tyler did it." He wouldn't even be in the room. He didn't understand blame yet, or how rules bent.

I sat them down. "You don't get to hide behind someone who can't fight back. He's your brother. Family protects each other."

Once, I came around the corner and found Thomas sitting cross-legged beside Tyler in total silence. Both boys were watching the ceiling fan spin, eyes tracing its lazy circles as if it held secrets. "What are you doing?" I whispered.

"Waiting," Thomas said, not looking up.

"For what?"

"Until he's ready."

They stayed there like that with no toys, no noise, no pressure. Just stillness shared between brothers. It wasn't therapy; it wasn't strategy. It was grace, the kind that children give without realizing its holy. They gave him what the world couldn't: time without expectation.

Miracles: The Small Holy Things

He didn't hit milestones. He hit memories.

A glance held for three seconds, then four.

A towel hung crookedly without a prompt.

We left two minutes late, and he didn't crumble; he hummed once and reached for my hand.

No balloons. No cake. Just quiet smiles across the room: Did you see that? He did it.

The Tooth Saga

Other moms mark first steps, first words, and first days of school. I marked Tyler's first hug, his first eye contact, and the first time he washed his hands without a bribe.

He lost his first tooth without recognition. I noticed the gap while brushing. No tooth in the sheets, none clenched in his fist. Just…gone. The tooth fairy still came, a crumpled dollar under his pillow. He looked wide-eyed and hummed but didn't connect the dots the way Jacob had.

The next tooth I caught in real time; I rinsed it for safekeeping. That's when he unraveled.

He wanted it back in.

He pointed to his mouth and cried, "Put it back." His words were few, but the meaning was clear: something important had fallen out, and he wasn't ready to lose it. He pressed the tooth into my palm, breath hitching. "Back," he begged.

We sat on the kitchen floor and breathed together (in two three, out two three) while I showed him a diagram of baby teeth from a book. I rolled a pea of bread dough and tucked it in the gap to "hold the place." Not science; comfort. His shoulders dropped. We wrapped the tooth in tissue and put it in a jar. "Keep safe," I promised. One fierce nod.

Through tears, he finally told me what happened to the first one. He'd tried to put it back. He swallowed it, believing his body could fix him from the inside.

That night was a duet of meltdowns; his from terror, mine from exhaustion. We ended in a forced hug: my arms around him while he screamed until his body softened against me. He understood enough not to swallow this one, even if he didn't believe me completely.

The next two teeth vanished. Hidden before I could see. Maybe he fed them back to his body in secret; maybe the backyard keeps them under the line of rocks he loved. I've made peace with the mystery. Not everything needs my label to be real.

My line in the sand started as defiance against systems, against ignorance, against exhaustion, but somewhere along the way it became faith. Faith that communication isn't always verbal. Faith that progress doesn't need to look like anyone else's graph. Faith that the bridge between us might not be made of words, but it holds all the same.

I stopped hearing, "When will he catch up?" and started asking, "Where can we restart?" Every day offered a new edge to press, a gentler doorway to try. He won't "max out." He'll keep restarting. And because I have him, so will I

Prayers and Meltdowns

Before the Storm

He won't "max out." He restarts. So, do I.

The house was never quiet. Not really. Even when Tyler wasn't screaming, I could feel it coming. Silence had weight that was unnatural and heavy like the pause before thunder. His pacing changed; his hands fluttered faster; the air vibrated. My body did the math without asking my brain: pillows, corners, doors that lock. A mother's silent inventory. Chest tight. Jaw clenched. Breath held.

And then it came.

Impact

The scream hit like a flare inside my skull. His body went steel; it was rigid and unyielding, then thrashed. A chair clattered. His heel slammed the cabinet; the bang ricocheted through the kitchen like gunfire.

I dropped to my knees. Arms around him the way the therapist taught: deep pressure, not too tight, not too loose. He writhed, voice tearing at walls and nerves and heart. His head snapped back, cracking my chin. I bit through my tongue. Blood tasted metallic and hot.

Still, I held.

He was so strong, unnaturally strong for a boy his size. My arms shook, muscles trembling. Each second was a calculation: shift left and miss the table leg; shift right and block the glass. I'd become a strategist in the middle of a storm.

Ten minutes. Fifteen. I stopped counting. Sweat ran down my back. His face purpled from screaming; his chest heaved; my arms went numb.

Knock

A soft rap at the door—polite, listening. Pause. A firmer knock.

"Everything okay in there?" a neighbor sang through the wood.

Shame burned hotter than sweat. What did she hear? The scream? My grunt? Furniture on tile?

I wanted to laugh and sob. Nothing was okay. I swallowed blood and said, "We're fine!"

It came out brittle, a glass word already cracked.

He wailed in my arms. I wondered if she believed me. I wondered how many knocks like that were in my future.

And then, like storms do, it ended. Calm replaced chaos. Tyler hummed softly, as if nothing had happened. My hands shook. Tears slid without sound; sound startled him. This wasn't a tantrum. This was survival.

Aftermath

After a meltdown, the house looked like a crime scene. Not because he'd done anything wrong, but because the storm leaves wreckage.

Cushions flung like debris. A chair tilted, a gouge down the floor. A lamp on its side, shade dented. Toys abandoned mid-play. Even the air felt dense, humming with echoes.

My body shook as if we had crashed into a car. Arms ached with phantom weight. Jaw throbbed. Shirt was damp and stretched from his grip. Ears rang in the quiet.

Tyler recovered first. While I was still gasping, he was curled under Nemo, his chest rising steadily. Small. Fragile. A soldier asleep after battle.

I sat nearby and brushed curls off his forehead. "You're safe now," I whispered. A ritual, part prayer, part mantra. Maybe if I said it enough, it would be true.

Then clean up. Lamp upright. Cushions smoothed. Blanket folded. Toys back in bins. Movements automatic, as if restoring the room could restore control. Red marks on my arms. A living room reassembled.

In the hallway mirror: a woman I barely knew, her hair wild, eyes hollow, shirt warped. Survival wears a face.

In the next room, life went on. Hailey was on her stomach, coloring with Justin. Thomas was rebuilding Legos with monk-like calm. Jacob was lost in a book. They adapted with grace I couldn't always find. It amazed me. It broke me.

Evening Rebuild

By evening, the house always softened again. Dinner simmered on the stove: spaghetti or boxed macaroni, whatever I could manage with one hand while the other kept order. The kids' laughter started to creep back in, cautious at first, then brighter.

Tyler would emerge from his room, hair sticking up, cheeks flushed, the hum trailing behind him like a faint melody. Jacob would slide a toy car across the floor toward him, a peace offering. Tyler would roll it back, slow and measured. Connection was rebuilt in the quietest of ways.

I'd stand at the sink, washing dishes, watching the exchange reflected in the window, the ghost of a mother framed against the night, a boy learning to trust the world again one matchbox car at a time.

Some nights I'd turn on music low, old country songs my dad used to play. Tyler didn't like the lyrics, but he loved the rhythm. He'd tap along, not quite on beat but perfectly himself. The others would join in, clapping off-time, turning the kitchen into something that almost felt like joy.

It wasn't peace, but it was close enough to borrow the word for a night.

Siblings at Night

Later, when the lights were out and the house had fallen into uneasy sleep, I'd hear the soft shuffle of little feet. The door creaked open and Jacob slipped in, his hair sticking up like static, eyes wide in the half-dark.

"Is he okay?" he'd whisper.

"He's okay," I whispered back.

He'd climb into my lap, too big for it but still needing it, and rest his head against my chest. We'd listen to the faint hum drifting from Tyler's room, a sound that meant peace had returned, at least for the night. Jacob never said much. He didn't have to. He carried his own version of the noise, the kind that doesn't scream but still echoes.

When he finally drifted off, I'd carry him back to bed, tuck the blanket under his chin, and think about how all of us were learning to survive the same war in different ways.

Then I heard it, Tyler's hum from the other room, soft and steady. His way of returning. Every time, it stood me back up.

Morning After

The next morning always carried the wrong kind of quiet: the heavy kind, the aftermath kind. The sun came up like it always did, but the house felt hollowed out. Tyler padded into the kitchen in footie pajamas, face unmarked, asking for waffles as if the night before had been erased.

My body disagreed. My arms ached; my jaw throbbed. I poured batter with shaking hands, pretending normal. Jacob hummed the same tune Tyler always used, soft and off-key, a peace offering disguised as music. The smell of syrup and burned edges filled the kitchen. Nobody mentioned the storm. We never did. Silence was our apology. Silence was the truce.

Sometimes, when I caught Tyler watching the waffle maker, eyes half-lidded with exhaustion, I wondered if he remembered any of it: the crash, the scream, the way my arms locked around him until we both shook. Maybe he did. Maybe he didn't. Maybe forgetting was mercy.

But my body remembered. Always.

Waiting

I lived on a fault line, waiting for a teacher's call, a scream, a stranger's stare. And praying. Always praying. Because no one tells you how isolating it is.

Even today you can't post, "I carried my child out of Target under my arm while strangers whispered." That doesn't get likes. It gets judgment. Back then there was no group for understanding or support; there was no meeting I could find comfort in knowing someone else held the same battle scars as I did. It was seven people under one roof trying to understand something the world still didn't care about.

The Market

I went in braced: groceries, socks, maybe one brave detour. "Please, God, let me make it through." Fluorescents buzzed like bees in glass. Tyler perched in the cart, rocking, Nemo blanket under his chin. The little ones argued about cereal mascots. It felt almost normal.

Every trip had a rhythm. Chips on the endcaps by the registers: always. Predictability in a world that didn't offer much.

That day, the chips were gone. Snack cakes took their place.

I saw it first. The air shifted. His humming stopped. His eyes widened.

"No," I whispered. "Not here."

Too late.

The scream sliced through the store. Heads turned. He kicked, ripped socks from a display, and flung them like white flags no one read. I pulled him from the cart and wrapped him tight. He thrashed, heels into my thighs, nails across my arm. From the outside, it must have looked brutal. People stared; some shook their heads; some steered clear like we were contagious.

I wanted to stand on the conveyor belt and shout, "This is not a tantrum." The chips moved. His world broke. But explanations don't land in the middle of sirens.

So, I carried him out.

One kid pushed the cart that held only children: another trailed, eyes down. In the car, I strapped him in as gently as shaking hands allowed. "You're safe, you're safe," I whispered into his hair while my voice frayed. His sobs hiccupped, then faded to a hum. For him, it was over. For me, it never was.

The Meeting

A few days after the market storm, I sat in a folding chair across from a preschool teacher who wouldn't meet my eyes. The room smelled like coffee and disinfectant, a smell I would come to associate with bureaucratic defeat. She gestured at the clipboard in front of her.

"Maybe he just needs more structure at home," she said gently, which is what people say when they want to blame you but still sound nice.

I nodded, the way women are trained to nod. My palms were damp, my tongue bitten raw from holding back the words that would make me sound "difficult." But something inside me (some primal, exhausted corner) snapped.

"We have structure," I said. "We live by structure. We breathe it. He doesn't need more of it. He needs someone who understands what happens when his world breaks."

She blinked. "It's just... disruptive for the other kids."

I smiled. The kind of smile that doesn't mean yes. "So is ignorance," I said.

I walked out shaking. I didn't know it then, but that was the day I stopped apologizing for my son. Every storm after that one, every public meltdown, every sideways glance, it all came with a little more steel in my spine. People would understand sensory sensitivities; they would learn our world if I had to tell them individually; somehow, people would learn to understand.

Applebee's

We stopped eating out for a long time. The stares were heavy; the whispers were sharp. Hope won once. Applebee's: not fancy, just a test.

I packed for battle: snacks, sippy cup, the Nemo blanket I'd sewn, edges worn soft. I don't know why it worked, maybe smell, maybe history. Probably because it was Jacob's. It was his shield. Mine too.

We chose the corner booth. I faced the door, calculating exit routes. Ten minutes of maybe. Jacob chattered about superheroes. Thomas chose a crayon. Justin and Hailey babbled their secret language. Tyler pressed into the wall, eyes tracking lights, humming steadily.

A glass slipped from a waiter's tray and shattered.

Tyler seized before sound; then screamed. The plate shoved and clattered to the floor. He vanished under the table, hands over ears, world ended.

The restaurant froze. Forks were suspended. A silence louder than his cry.

I slid under the table and pulled the blanket over his head. Rough carpet burned my knees. "You're safe, baby. You're safe." Above us, whispers:

"Tantrum."

"Can't they control him?"

"What's wrong with that kid?"

Stones with voices. I stayed under the table and rocked him while strangers judged. Explaining wouldn't change anything.

When the storm passed, he sagged, hiccupping, sweat-damp. I crawled out, shielding him. The food sat untouched; the stares followed us to the door. In the car, the hum returned. My dignity stayed under that booth, folded into shadow.

Therapy Season

ABA. Speech. OT. My calendar turned into a rainbow of appointments: neat boxes that looked like progress and felt like quicksand. Every day, another specialist, another chart, another promise that work equals breakthroughs.

Tyler hated most of it. Flashcards were traps. Schedules became cages. Some days he tolerated drills, body tense but compliant. Other days he bolted on small legs faster than anyone had expected.

Still, I clung white-knuckled. Sometimes there were flickers: a point to a picture, a new sound. Two steps forward, one meltdown back. Tangled progress.

Library Research

When therapy didn't give me enough answers, I went hunting for my own. The library became my battleground.

I'd place the kids in the children's corner with board books and snacks. I'd pray no one noticed the crumbs or noise. Then, I'd sit at a public computer, my heart racing as if I were stealing secrets. I'd type autism regression into the search bar, and the screen would fill with a language I didn't yet speak, studies, journals, foreign terms that all boiled down to the same sentence: we don't know why.

Still, I printed everything I could afford. Fifty cents bought me five pages of hope. I highlighted every line that sounded remotely familiar: sensory processing, stimming, nonverbal, dyspraxia. I underlined hopeful phrases until the ink bled through.

Some days, I'd look up and realize the boys were asleep on the rug, Jacob's arm slung protectively over Tyler's chest. The librarian would pass by glance at the stack of printouts beside me, and smile politely, the kind of smile people give when they don't understand but wish they did.

I'd stuff the papers into my binder, my "Bible of the Unknown," and whisper small promises to myself: I will learn this language. I will translate my child to the world if it kills me.

At night, when I read those same pages by the light of the cheap lamp, the words blurred together until I stopped seeing text and only saw Tyler, his hands fluttering, his eyes searching. The scientists talked about "behaviors." I saw survival.

Waiting Room

Every waiting room had the same smell: disinfectants, dry marker, fear. Parents sat side by side, pretending to read outdated magazines while sneaking glances at each other's children.

I learned to spot the newcomers, the hopeful ones still clinging to the idea that this was just a "phase." They filled out forms with neat handwriting and nervous smiles. Then there were the veterans like me, binder in lap, eyes flat with fatigue, hope sharpened into armor.

We rarely spoke, but when we did, it was shorthand.

"How old?"

"Four."

"Nonverbal?"

"Mostly."

A nod. A shared exhale. An invisible community of the unseen.

Sometimes, a mother would cry quietly beside me while her child screamed down the hall. I'd pass her a tissue without a word, the universal offering of women who've been there. No one judged. We'd all been the mother in the hallway once, the one restraining, pleading, apologizing to strangers for a storm we didn't summon.

I used to envy the moms who got to complain about picky eaters and forgotten homework. Now I just envied silence. But every time I watched Tyler through the therapy window, his small hands gripping a toy car, his mouth shaping almost words, something in me unclenched.

He wasn't broken. He was building. And I would keep showing up until the world learned to see that, too.

Use Your Words

The speech toys smelled like disinfectants. Toys were used to teach, not to play. Tyler sat in the tiny chair with the Nemo blanket balled in his lap.

The therapist's smile was too bright. She slid a laminated board across. "Use your words," she said, tapping pictures with a manicured nail. "Which one? Show me."

He stared. Fingers twitched. Lips parted. No sound. Panic climbed; fists clenched; breath went ragged. He wasn't refusing. He was drowning.

From the corner, Thomas spoke, his small legs dangling, voice steady. "He wants the ball," he said, daring any adult to disagree.

"He needs to tell us," The therapist said.

"He doesn't need to," Thomas said louder. "I already know."

Tyler's eyes flicked to his brother. His body softened. He reached for the ball greedily, no board, no script, no point, and no words.

Pride and heartbreak braided in my chest. No manual captures that bond or tells you how to nurture it without making the sibling carry too much.

The therapist wrote something down. Another note for another chart. The only data that mattered was the look between my boys: I'll speak when you can't. This would go in the win tab of my binder.

Fruit Snacks

There was a fruit snack day.

It sounds small and ridiculous, unless you've lived it. Tyler had the same routine every single morning. He'd get his fruit snacks right before Fairly OddParents came on, and I always opened them the same way: down the long side, so he could reach in and pull them out one by one.

One morning, his dad was home and trying to help. He grabbed the pack, tore it open across the short side with his teeth, and handed it to Tyler like it was no big deal. But in Tyler's world, that single rip changed everything.

He froze. Then he screamed. And screamed again. His entire day unraveled before my eyes, a perfect storm from something as small as the direction of a tear.

To anyone else, it was just fruit snacks. To Tyler, it was order, safety, and the rhythm that kept his world predictable. When that pattern broke, so did his peace.

Nothing else got done that day. Not therapy, not errands, not even lunch. Just the echo of a meltdown that started with good intentions and ended with silence, the kind of silence that feels heavier than the noise ever did.

Later that night, when the house finally went still, I sat on the edge of the bed and prayed not for the day to be easier, but for the strength to keep showing up when it wasn't. Because that's what parenting Tyler was: a thousand tiny moments that could go right or wrong with the tear of a wrapper. Every meltdown felt like a failure at first, until I started realizing that it wasn't about control; it was about understanding. The prayers weren't to fix him. They were to remind me that love was bigger than the chaos.

Marriage Fracture

Meltdowns didn't just crack walls. They cracked marriages.

After one particularly brutal night, a two-hour storm that ended with both of us sobbing on opposite sides of Tyler's bedroom door, I found myself sitting at the kitchen table while Dad stared at the floor. The clock ticked too loudly. The hum of the refrigerator filled the silence between us.

He rubbed the back of his neck and said, "Maybe you're too soft on him."

Something inside me splintered. "Too soft?" I whispered. "You try holding him when he's terrified of his own skin."

"I'm trying," he said, voice flat. "We're all trying."

We sat there, two ghosts haunting the same kitchen, both exhausted, both right, both wrong. The distance between us wasn't measured in feet. It was measured in hours of sleep lost, in screams absorbed by drywall, in the way we both loved our son but couldn't always love each other the same way anymore.

That night, when he went to bed, I stayed in the dark, elbows on the table, forehead pressed to my hands. I didn't cry. I was too tired for that. Instead, I whispered another small prayer, not for miracles, but for the strength to keep choosing family even when it felt impossible.

Love didn't feel like candlelight dinners anymore. It felt like two people holding opposite ends of the same rope, refusing to let go. Somewhere along the way, I stopped being a wife and just became a mother and advocate. It was how it had to be, how I had to be. I had so much guilt because I did not nurse Tyler, because maybe I was quirky, socially distant, and sometimes emotionally cold, and maybe I really did teach him to be this way. The only way to ease my guilt was to be the perfect mother and advocate. There was nothing left in me to give as a wife; everything went to my kids and autism.

Bathroom Prayers

Night, when the house finally stilled, I locked myself in the bathroom; the only room with a door I could control.

Cold tile seeped into bone. Sometimes I didn't turn on the light. I sat in the doorway's spill, knees to chest, arms wrapped tight like I needed restraining. The hum of the baby monitor was present. A floorboard creaked. Tyler turned, a faint hum even in sleep. I listened and tried to breathe.

Prayers came thin as a thread. "Please let him sleep."

"Please, God, one easy day."

"Make me soft when I want to scream."

Some nights I bargained my sleep for his calm. Some nights there were no words, only tears darkening pajama cotton. I didn't pray for a cure or a different child. I prayed for survival, patience, a gentler voice, and enough love left for morning.

The bathroom was a sanctuary and confessional. I'd splash cold water on my face. I'd meet the mirror's stranger: mascara streaks, swollen eyes. Then, I'd straighten up anyway. Unlock the door. Step back into noise as if nothing broke. I was twenty-five but felt like I had lived three lifetimes.

Faith and Fire

Faith changed shape that year. It stopped looking like sermons or hymns. It became something feral and private, something that lived in the space between exhaustion and surrender. My prayers weren't elegant. They came out cracked, half-formed, like the gasps of someone treading water.

I stopped praying for peace. I prayed for persistence. For the ability to keep loving through the noise, through the bruises, through the days that ended with both of us on the floor.

Sometimes I thought about Mary, the sanitized version from church paintings, blue robe untouched, face serene. I wondered what the real Mary looked like at three in the morning when her child wouldn't sleep. I wondered if she ever screamed into a pillow, if she ever begged God for silence. Faith, I decided, wasn't serenity. It was showing up anyway.

What We Celebrate

Those years were prayer and meltdowns. Bargains with God and with myself. Bruises on walls, on heart, sometimes on skin. Charts that looked neat and crumbled in real life.

The world wanted Tyler boxed: diagnoses, statistics, milestones. He never fit. He refused to be measured that way.

So we celebrated what most mothers miss.

A single new word whispered like a miracle.

A night he slept, and I did too.

A storm that lasted fifteen minutes instead of thirty.

The soft hum against my chest when I swore I was empty.

Siblings carry on with a resilience that most adults never master.

No balloons. No applause. Grit. His. Mine. Our family's. The kind that digs in when the sky turns and refuses to let go.

And prayer. Always prayer. After the wreckage cleared, two things remained: the hum of my boy returning and the whispered prayers that carried us both through fire.

Some nights, when the hum finally quieted and the house exhaled, I'd sit on the edge of my bed and listen to the silence like a heartbeat. The prayers, the meltdowns, the wreckage, they weren't opposites. They were the same thing: the sound of a mother and a child refusing to give up on each other. That's what grace really was. Not peace. Persistence.

The First "I Love You"

Silence

For years, I carried silence like a second skin.

Back then, he was just three, but I felt one hundred.

Therapists called it nonverbal. Doctors said delayed. Strangers called it bad parenting. What I called it was lonely. Because there is nothing lonelier than pouring love into a child who cannot (or will not) speak it back.

The Grind

So we worked. God, did we work.

Speech therapy twice a week; ABA five days a week. Early intervention visits in our living room, laminated picture cards scattered across the carpet like confetti no one celebrated. Every session felt like running a marathon just to move an inch.

"Point to the apple."

"Say ball."

"Say hi."

Sometimes he screamed. Sometimes he spun. Sometimes he just stared straight through the therapist like she didn't exist. We tried sticker charts, songs, candy, and timers. Nothing came easy.

Drills

The living room always turned into a stage when therapy started.

A mat spread across the carpet, cards stacked neatly on the coffee table, and a timer set on the side. Tyler perched stiffly in his little chair, his fingers tapping the edge, eyes darting anywhere but at the therapist.

"Say ball," she prompted, holding up a bright red ball from the bin.

Tyler flinched, his gaze sliding past her face.

"Ball," she repeated, slower this time, her smile fixed but strained. She tapped the picture card with her manicured nail. "Tyler, say it. Ball."

He shifted in his seat, whining low in his throat. His hands went to his ears.

"Ball," she said again, sharper now, like the word itself would break him open if she forced it hard enough.

He screamed.

It was a raw, piercing sound that filled the room and rattled through my chest. His little body arched, then crumpled to the floor. He spun in a tight circle, fists slamming against his head, tears streaking down his face.

The therapist scribbled notes on her clipboard, glancing at her watch. She marked something in her chart — noncompliant, prompted three times, no response.

But she didn't write what I saw.

She didn't write how his chest heaved, how the cords in his neck stood out, how his fists left red marks on his own skin. She didn't write how I sat cross-legged on the floor across the room, biting the inside of my cheek so hard I tasted blood, digging my fingernails into my palm so I wouldn't cry in front of her.

When the timer finally beeped, she sighed, straightened her papers, and smiled that too-bright smile. "We'll try again next time."

And just like that, she was gone.

Questions

The silence that followed wasn't peace; it was wreckage.

Flashcards were scattered across the floor, half-bent from Tyler's fists. The timer still blinked on the coffee table, long since expired. The air smelled like sweat and tears mixed with Lysol wipes.

I knelt to start the ritual cleanup. Stacking cards. Putting toys back in bins. Folding the therapy mat and sliding it behind the couch like it was a secret I wanted hidden. My movements were slow, mechanical, the way you move when your body's gone numb.

Tyler had already retreated into his corner, humming softly, rocking in rhythm with the ceiling fan. His storm had passed, and just like that, he was calm again, oblivious to the way my body still shook.

Jacob, though, wasn't oblivious. He climbed into my lap as I gathered the last stack of cards and asked in his tiny voice, "Why does TyTy scream so much?"

I swallowed hard. How do you explain sensory overload, frustration, and a body that feels like a prison to a five-year-old? I kissed the top of his head and whispered, "Because the world feels too big for him sometimes."

Jacob seemed to accept that, nodding solemnly, then asked, "Can I help it feel small again?" The weight of that broke me. He was only a child, yet he already wanted to carry some of the load.

Later, when all the boys were finally asleep, I sat in the quiet living room and stared at the folded mat peeking out from behind the couch. All I could think about was how much of our home and our lives had been reshaped by therapy. Our family was living inside someone else's system: token boards, timers, drills, charts.

They told me this was progress. But sitting there in the wreckage, I wondered if we were moving forward or just spinning in circles, like Tyler had earlier on the floor.

That's when the guilt came. Crushing, relentless. Was I doing enough? Was I pushing too hard? Did Tyler need more sessions, or fewer? Did he hate me for putting him through this?

I carried those questions with me to bed that night, heavy as stones.

And when the baby monitor crackled with Tyler's restless hum hours later, I knew tomorrow would be another round. Another storm. Another cleanup. Another night of questions without answers.

Progress was so slow it felt like crawling across broken glass.

Becoming a Therapist

And somewhere in that grind, I became the therapist, too.

Our home stopped feeling like a home. The couch was shoved against the wall to make room for therapy mats. Shelves sagged with bins of flashcards, token boards, and laminated charts. A timer sat on the coffee table, always ticking down to another drill. The air smelled faintly of Clorox wipes and burnt coffee: my survival staples.

There were days when the house was full of people: therapists, early interventionists, specialists, and yet I'd never felt more alone. Tyler would scream as they tried to coax him into naming objects. Sometimes he'd go limp on the floor, refusing to engage. Other days he'd spin in tight, dizzying circles while the therapist scribbled notes on a clipboard like she was logging a specimen instead of a little boy.

I'd sit frozen, biting my tongue so hard I tasted blood because I knew the data sheets mattered. I knew every "prompt level" counted. I knew the world would not bend for Tyler, so I had to teach him to bend for it, even if it broke me.

When the therapists left, it was just me and Tyler. And the silence.

I'd sit cross-legged on the carpet, exhausted, running the drills myself. Jacob climbed furniture in the background. Thomas cried in his swing. I sipped cold coffee and pressed picture cards into Tyler's hand.

"Say ball."

"Say apple."

Sometimes he looked right through me.

I'd excuse myself to the bathroom, close the door, and cry silently. Then wipe my face, take a deep breath, and come back out like nothing happened. Because if I quit, who else would fight for him?

Lifelines

But there were people who believed, even in the grind. And they didn't just believe in Tyler. They believed in us.

The first time we went to the pumpkin patch with Mrs. M's class, I carried dread in my chest. Outings always ended in meltdowns or stares. But the moment we stepped onto that field, I knew something was different.

Kids darted between pumpkins, spinning, stimming, laughing in their own rhythms, and no one flinched. Parents chatted without whispering about "that child." For once, we weren't the family on the outside looking in.

At the pumpkin patch, Tyler bent down to pick up his lopsided pumpkin, and his shoelace trailed into the dirt. Normally, he hated anyone touching him, but when Mrs. M crouched beside him and quietly tied his shoe, he didn't pull away.

It wasn't about the shoelace; it was about the way she saw him. No lecture. No sigh. Just a gentle act that said, I'll meet you where you are.

I stood there stunned. To anyone else, it looked like nothing. But to me, it was everything. Because it wasn't just a teacher tying a shoe. It was an adult outside of our family showing patience with my son on his terms.

He ran over, shoes safe, and began to inspect all the pumpkins.

He crouched low, running his hands over every pumpkin in sight, tapping their surfaces, humming softly. He paused at a small, lopsided one and patted it like he had discovered treasure. Jacob rushed over, puffing his chest as he scooped it up.

"I'll carry it, Ty!" he announced, staggering a little under the weight.

Tyler didn't say a word, but he let Jacob walk beside him; the two of them wobbled together back toward me.

I stood in the crisp October air, paper cup of cider warming my hand, new baby strapped to my chest, tears stinging my eyes. For the first time in years, I wasn't the mom being stared at. I was just a mom, holding cider, watching her kids pick pumpkins.

We went with Mrs. M's class three years in a row. Even now, I can't step into a pumpkin patch without thinking of her.

And then there was Mr. J

Mr. J was the kind of teacher every parent dreams of, the one who looks at every child as a whole person. He didn't just tolerate quirks; he celebrated them. He knew Tyler didn't always thrive in a structured setting, so he worked with him instead of against him.

Kite Day at the elementary school was loud and chaotic, two things Tyler usually couldn't stand. The sky stretched Carolina blue, the wind sharp, kids yelling as kites tangled in midair.

Tyler's anxiety was climbing. His hands pressed to his ears, his body rocking on the edge of the field. I braced myself for a meltdown.

Then Mr. J knelt down beside him, calm as ever, and placed the kite string in Tyler's hands. His big teacher's hands wrapped gently around my son's small ones.

"Ready?" he asked.

Tyler didn't answer, but he didn't pull away.

Together they ran, and the kite jerked, lifted, and soared. The second it caught the wind, Tyler's whole body changed. His eyes widened, his mouth opened in a burst of laughter, real laughter, bubbling up from someplace deep.

When the kite finally swooped down, trailing across the grass, Tyler dropped the string and looked up at Mr. J, uncertain.

Without hesitation, Mr. J held up his hand. "High five, champ!"

Tyler hesitated at first, then slapped his palm against his teacher's. His face broke into a grin so wide it felt like the sun had come out all over again.

It was such a simple thing, but I felt tears sting in my eyes. So many adults looked at Tyler's quirks with impatience or pity. Mr. J looked at him like a boy worth celebrating.

I froze, stunned by the sound. Dad and I could not believe it.

Mr. J grinned, steadying the line as Tyler jumped and squealed, pulling the string with all his might. Then he turned to me, still laughing, and pressed a kite into my hands.

"Your turn, Mom."

I hadn't run like that in years. Hair whipping, chest heaving, the kite straining against my grip. And I laughed; I really laughed. For those few minutes, I wasn't bracing for judgment. I wasn't just surviving. I was Jacqueline, a mom, flying a kite.

That man gave me the gift of breathing again.

Ms. M taught Jacob in kindergarten, but her love stretched to all of my boys.

On the hardest days, when Tyler couldn't manage his own classroom, she let him slip into hers. No forms. No fuss. Just an open chair next to his brother. Jacob would beam with pride, patting the seat beside him. Tyler would hum softly, safe in the buzz of crayons scratching and kids chattering.

No one teased. No one questioned. Because Ms. M had already set the tone: everyone belonged.

Later, she taught Justin too, giving him the same gentle patience she gave Tyler. Even Thomas, who never sat in her class, found himself under her watchful eye.

She didn't just teach academics. She taught belonging. She taught love.

Looking back, those three, M, J, and M, weren't just educators. They were lifelines. They gave us hope when the world was loud and judgmental. They saw my son as a child first, not a challenge to fix. They welcomed our whole family with open arms, gave my kids a place to belong, and gave me a moment to rest my shoulders.

When I think about those early years, I don't just remember the meltdowns or the exhaustion. I remember Mrs. M crouched down in a pumpkin field helping Tyler choose his favorite. I remember Mr. J grinning like a proud parent as Tyler's kite climbed higher and higher. I remember Ms. M letting Tyler sneak into Jacob's classroom so he could be near his brother.

2009

It was 2009. Dad had been home for a while, but the shadow of deployments clung to him like dust on boots. He had missed so many firsts, first steps, first birthdays, milestones I tried to preserve in shaky photos and grainy videos. But deep down, we both knew what he longed for most: to hear his son say, "I love you."

Jacob was 6 now, in first grade; Tyler was four, Thomas had just turned three, Justin was still rocking footie pajamas while Hailey grew in my belly.

A nighttime ritual had been born through Dr. Seuss.

That night wasn't special. Pajamas and bedtime chaos. Me folding laundry in the hallway, the dryer humming its steady rhythm. Dad on the couch with the kids, same as always.

Tyler's obsession at the time was Green Eggs and Ham. He giggled wildly at the rhymes, laughing harder when Dad exaggerated the voices. For a few minutes, the house felt light.

Maybe that's why it happened, because no one was forcing it. No flashcards. No token boards. Just a boy, his dad, and a storybook.

I stood in the hallway, a towel in my hands, half-listening as Dad's voice carried through the door.

"I do not like them, Sam-I-Am…"

Tyler's laughter bubbled up, sharp and clear.

Then Dad's tone shifted. Softer. More tentative.

"I love you, buddy."

The room went still. A pause so heavy it felt like the air thickened.

Tyler looked up. His eyes met his father's… steady, unblinking. And then, in halting words, barely above a whisper:

"Tyler love Daddy."

The towel slipped from my hands. My breath caught like I'd been struck. Dad froze, then crumpled, scooping his son into his arms, clutching him as though the words themselves might vanish.

I stood in the doorway, tears flooding my face, chest aching so hard it was almost painful. Years of silence, years of questions, years of prayers cracked open in that single heartbeat.

"Tyler love Daddy."

You cannot understand the weight of those words unless you've lived without them. Unless you've poured love into silence for years, wondering if it ever landed. Unless you've prayed night after night just for your child to look at you, to see you.

That night, Tyler saw.

When the words left his mouth, "Tyler love Daddy" time didn't just slow; it split wide open.

For a moment, none of us moved. The room held its breath. Dad clutched him, rocking like the harder he held on, the less chance those words could slip away.

I stood in the doorway, frozen, hands trembling, the towel at my feet. My vision blurred, but I couldn't blink. I was terrified that if I moved, the spell would break.

Eventually, Tyler squirmed, wriggling free from Dad's arms. Just like that, he went back to flipping pages, tracing the pictures with his finger, as if he hadn't just cracked our world in two.

But Dad didn't move. He sat on the edge of the couch with his face in his hands, shoulders shaking. The soldier who had stood tall through deployments, who had faced desert heat and endless nights away from us, was undone by three small words.

I crossed the room and sank beside him. Neither of us spoke. There was nothing to say. We sat there together in the dim light of the lamp, watching our son hum and flip pages, pretending we hadn't just been changed forever.

Later that night, when the house was quiet, we sat at the kitchen table, cups of coffee cooling between us. I remember staring at the steam curling upward, whispering, "He said it. He really said it."

Dad's eyes were red, his voice rough. "I could die tomorrow, and I'd be okay. Because I heard him say it."

That night, I realized those three words weren't just proof of love. They were proof of survival. That everything we had clawed through (the therapy, the meltdowns, the silence) had not been in vain.

The Morning After

The next morning, the house felt different. Lighter, somehow, though maybe it was just me.

I padded down the hall, heart thudding in my chest, half-afraid the night before had been a dream. Tyler was already awake, perched on the edge of his bed, flipping the same worn copy of Green Eggs and Ham. He didn't look up when I came in.

I sat beside him, close but not touching, and whispered, "Good morning, buddy."

He hummed softly, eyes on the pages. No words. Not yet.

For a split second, disappointment stabbed through me. I had to remind myself that those three words weren't a faucet to turn on and off. They were a gift. And gifts don't arrive on demand.

In the kitchen, Dad sat hunched over his mug of coffee, elbows on the table. His eyes were red from crying, though he would never admit it.

He looked at me, his voice low. "Do you think he will say it again?"

I didn't answer right away. Because the truth was, I didn't know. A part of me was terrified it had been a once-in-a-lifetime spark, something we'd spend years chasing but never hear again.

Finally, I said, "I don't know. But he said it once. That means it's in there."

We sat in silence, both holding onto the memory like it was porcelain: fragile, breakable, too precious to set down.

And that became the rhythm of the days that followed: waiting, listening, hoping. Every laugh, every hum, every glance carried the question, will he say it again?

Years Later

It would be years later before he saw me, too.

By then, I was newly divorced. Tyler was almost eight, and we were living in a house with roommates. It wasn't glamorous, hand-me-down furniture, kids' clothes always in laundry baskets, and too many schedules overlapping. But the backyard was magic. A trampoline. A treehouse. Space to breathe.

On my one rare day off that week, I spent it all with the kids. We jumped until our legs gave out, collapsing into a heap on the trampoline, sweaty and breathless. The air smelled of sunscreen and fresh-cut grass. The fabric beneath us radiated the day's heat.

Jacob and Thomas bounced on their knees, hiccupping from laughter. Tyler lay flat on his back, chest heaving, staring up at the wide stretch of blue sky. His hair stuck to his forehead with sweat. His lips curved into a rare, unguarded grin.

He turned toward me, eyes crinkling, and said it:

"Tyler loves Mommy."

Just like that. No prompt. No flashcard. No therapist. Just his voice in the open air.

When the words tumbled out, "Tyler love Mommy" I froze.

But Jacob didn't. He gasped so loudly I thought the neighbors might hear. His hands flew to his mouth and then shot straight into the air like he was celebrating a touchdown.

"Mommy! He said it! He said he loves you!" he shouted, bouncing so hard the trampoline nearly launched us all.

Thomas squealed and clapped, his little body hiccupping with giggles. "TyTy love Mommy!" he echoed, chanting it like a cheer. Justin and Hailey came running over to see what it the screaming and cheers were all about.

Their joy came in waves, spilling out, wrapping around me just as tight as Tyler's words had. They hadn't been waiting for therapists' charts or milestone checklists. They had been waiting for their brother to see me, to see us, the way we saw him every single day.

I pulled Tyler against me, burying my face in his damp hair, tears streaming down my cheeks. He squirmed after a few seconds, wiggling free to chase the laughter, already bouncing again. But the younger boys stayed pressed close, their little faces glowing with pride, as if they had been given the gift too. "Mommy love Tyler too"

I realized then it wasn't just my moment. It belonged to all of us. Every sibling who had sat through therapy sessions, waited through meltdowns, and carried quiet burdens too heavy for their age. They had been waiting too. And Tyler's words were theirs as much as they were mine.

The words hit me so hard I couldn't breathe. Tears blurred the sky. My chest shook.

The first "I love you" had been a whisper in a quiet room, fragile and halting. This one was a shout painted across the sky, free, joyful, loud.

Small Miracles

Both were miracles.

Now he tells me often. Sometimes scripted, sometimes pure. I don't care. Because when you wait eight years to hear it, the words are sweeter than any milestone.

I may never dance with him at his wedding. I may never hand him the keys to a first car. I don't know what the future holds, and I've stopped trying to force it into the shape I once imagined.

I do know this: nothing, and I mean nothing, will ever compare to the boy I was told would never speak saying, "Tyler love Mommy."

For years, silence wrapped itself around me like a second skin. It weighed me down. It made me invisible. It convinced me that maybe love wasn't reaching him at all.

But that day on the trampoline, the silence cracked. His words split it wide open, and the love I had poured out for years finally came echoing back.

It wasn't just Tyler who restarted. It was me too.

Because love doesn't always arrive the way you expect it to. Sometimes it's delayed. Sometimes it hides behind silence. Sometimes it takes years to surface.

But when it does come, whether whispered in a quiet room or shouted under an open sky, it changes everything

The Jumping Years

Jump

"Jump. Jump. Jump."

It was Tyler's favorite word. Sometimes shouted, sometimes whispered, sometimes chanted like a prayer. He said it when he was happy, when he was anxious, when he was spinning, and when he was still. *Jump jump jump.*

Jumping wasn't just play; it was survival. His body craved the rhythmic pounding of motion to feel anchored. Other kids bounced for fun. Tyler bounced to stay regulated, to keep his mind tethered, to survive the chaos of a world that often made no sense to him.

But the trampoline wasn't just a toy; it was his lifeline. The mat smelled faintly of sun and rubber, warm even in winter from the endless pounding of his feet. When he jumped, curls flying, the world snapped into rhythm. Each thud was an exhale, each bounce a reset. Sometimes I wondered if I should be jumping too; maybe then I'd find my balance the way he did. We would move it around the house, the yard, and even take it with us sometimes.

Literal

That was Tyler: literal to his bones. If you said "jump," he jumped. If the schedule said "snack," it had to be snack. There was no middle ground. The world was rules and commands and routines carved in stone. And somehow, we learned to live inside those rules with him. If you said "Go, Tyler, go," he would want to go. The rules didn't stop at words. They spilled into food, play, clothes, everything. Each part of his day came with its own script, and breaking even one line could unravel the whole scene.

Waiting Rooms

When we left the house without it, I braced myself. Waiting rooms were the worst. One time at the pediatrician's office, (the required fish tank in the corner that was supposed to be calming) Tyler pressed his body against the glass and bounced like the floor itself might turn into a trampoline if he pushed hard enough. When it didn't, he screamed: loud, guttural, unrelenting. Other parents shifted in their seats, whispering and clutching their kids closer.

I tried to scoop him up, but his body thrashed with all the strength of a child desperate for regulation. His feet kicked, his head slammed into my chest, and all I could do was hold on while the receptionist pretended not to stare.

Eventually, we ended up on the bathroom floor, the only private place I could find. Tyler bounced against the wall, pounding his heels, chanting *"Jump, jump, jump"* through sobs until his body gave out. When it was finally quiet, I wiped his face, smoothed his curls, and whispered, "Almost home, buddy. Almost to your trampoline."

That's when I realized the trampoline wasn't optional. It wasn't something I could limit or tuck away in a playroom. It was survival.

House Soundtrack

Our house echoed with the soundtrack of those years: the squeak of trampoline springs, the slap of his feet against the mat, and the thud-thud-thud of his landing shaking the living room floor. His trampoline wasn't tucked away outside anymore; it lived in the middle of the chaos because Tyler needed it constantly. Some days, he'd jump for a few minutes and reset. Other days, he'd jump until his curls stuck to his sweaty forehead and his little chest heaved, red-faced and determined.

One afternoon, I made the mistake of saying, "Oh, jump, Tyler Jump!" As the kids were using pillowcases as parachutes and jumping off the couch in a burst of silliness.

Before I could blink, he sprinted to the trampoline and started bouncing like he was fueled by rocket fuel. Over and over. One hundred jumps. Two hundred. The sound reverberated through the house, rhythmic and relentless. At first, we laughed, amused by his determination. Then we stared. Then we worried. Would he stop? He didn't, not until his body gave out, and he collapsed in a sweaty heap on the carpet, completely spent but utterly calm.

Food Rules

Tyler had favorite things, favorite foods, and favorite hobbies. For a long time, food was what we created our schedule around. His hyper fixation of the season would often change, but his love for raw veggies has never stopped. Especially broccoli.

Tyler's love of broccoli was one of his most enduring quirks. Not cookies. Not candy. Broccoli. Steamed, plain, served by the head if I let him. People thought it was adorable. "Oh, how healthy!" they'd laugh, imagining a picture-perfect kid who loved vegetables. They didn't see the meltdowns when we ran out or the way he'd fall apart if the florets weren't cooked just right; they never saw what happened when the broccoli was gone.

One evening, I had miscalculated. Dinner was ready, plates set, but when I opened the fridge, the produce drawer was empty. No broccoli. My stomach sank because I already knew what was coming.

When I set his plate down without the familiar pile of green florets, Tyler froze. His eyes darted to the space on the plate, scanning, searching, then back to me. He shoved the plate hard enough that noodles flew across the table. His body stiffened; his voice cracked open into a scream.

"BROCCOLI!"

It wasn't just a request. It was grief, panic, and fury all wrapped into one. He screamed until his cheeks were blotchy, throwing himself onto the floor and hitting his fists against the tile. Jacob sat wide-eyed, clutching his fork, while Thomas crawled under the table to hide from the storm.

I tried to soothe him, whispering, "I'll get more tomorrow, buddy. It's okay." But logic meant nothing in that moment. His world had lost one of its anchors, and nothing could right it until the ritual was restored.

That night, I learned to buy broccoli in bulk. Always three bags. Always cooked just right. Because running out wasn't just inconvenient; it was catastrophic.

Sometimes cooking them at all was one of the seven deadly sins.

Broccoli also gave us one of our best family jokes.

It happened during one of those chaotic evenings when everything feels like it's falling apart. I was trying to coax Tyler to eat more than just his broccoli while also yelling at Thomas, who had scaled the table for the fiftieth time that day. Exhausted and overwhelmed, my mom brain glitched. Out came:

"Broccoli, get down!"

Tyler burst into laughter so hard he couldn't breathe. He laughed until his face turned red, tears running down his cheeks. From that night on, "BROCCOLI!" became my cue, and "GET DOWN!" was his punchline. He'd yell it gleefully, then dissolve into giggles. Even now, as an adult, that simple phrase can still crack him open with belly laughter.

The Good Sauce

Spaghetti night was another battle. Tyler loved pasta but despised tomato chunks with the passion of a food critic. Honestly, I think Jacob started it; he hated them, too, but Tyler elevated it into an all-out war. For him, it wasn't just a preference. It was a deal breaker.

So, night after night, I stood at the counter, painstakingly straining every jar of sauce, spooning out tomato bits one by one like I was performing delicate surgery. It was tedious, ridiculous, and exhausting. But it was necessary.

Eventually, I hit a breaking point. I wasn't going to strain another jar of sauce at midnight. If this was going to be our life, I needed a better solution. So, I decided to learn how to make spaghetti sauce from scratch.

The early attempts were disasters. Burnt batches that left the kitchen smelling like charred garlic. Bland batches that tasted like nothing but disappointment. Over-seasoned batches that could've cleared your sinuses with one bite. But I kept going. Slowly, over months and years, I figured it out. The kitchen became my battlefield, sauce splatters on the wall like tiny red flags, wooden spoon as my weapon of choice. The smell of garlic and steam mixed with the sound of cartoons in the background, Thomas clattering toys on the floor while Jacob chattered at my elbow, and Justin and Hailey ran amok.

One day, I nailed it: a sauce that was rich, smooth, simple, and exactly the way Tyler needed it. That sauce became Tyler's sauce. To this day, the teens will ask me, "Mom, is this the good sauce?" Everyone in the family brags about it now, but the truth is, it only exists because of him. What once felt like endless frustration turned into a family staple. It was love disguised as a recipe, proof that connection sometimes comes not in big breakthroughs, but in the quiet persistence of making the world softer for your child, one bowl of spaghetti at a time. That lesson followed me everywhere: patience as a practice, not a virtue. If I could stand over a simmering pot and stir for hours until the flavors blended, maybe I could learn to wait out the hard moments too.

Potty Training

Those years were full of contradictions. Moments that made me cry from exhaustion and then laugh until my stomach hurt. Potty training, for example, felt like a never-ending war.

We tried everything: sticker charts, timers, candy bribes, backyard practice sessions, therapist data sheets. Progress looked neat and tidy on paper, but in real life it meant soaked carpets, a mountain of laundry at 2 a.m., and nights where I sat on the cold bathroom floor, head in my lap trying to figure out what would motivate him. One night stands out in my memory like a scar. It was 2 a.m., and the bathroom light burned harsh and bright against my exhausted eyes. Tyler sat on his little training seat, legs swinging, eyes fixed on the shampoo bottles he had lined up on the edge of the tub.

I'd been in there with him for almost an hour. The tile was cold under my legs as I slumped against the wall, chin resting on my knees, whispering encouragement that felt more like begging.

"You can do it, buddy. Just try."

He hummed softly, tapping the bottles one by one like a conductor checking his orchestra. The pull of his ritual was stronger than my words.

Outside the door, Jacob knocked with the impatience of a little boy who also needed to use the bathroom. "Mommy? Are you done yet?"

"Not yet, baby," I called back, my voice cracking.

By the time Tyler finally stood up and padded back to bed, I was left with nothing but a damp pull-up, a cold floor, and the sinking weight of failure. I sat there long after he left, staring at the shampoo bottles lined up in perfect order, wondering how much longer I could do this.

Those were the moments no sticker chart could capture.

I felt like I was failing him. Failing myself. Failing the rest of the kids who needed me too.

Then one day, he just… did it. No fanfare, no reward. He simply sat, went, and walked away like it was nothing. That was Tyler. Everything felt impossible until suddenly it wasn't. I still think it was because Thomas was potty training at the same time and he clicked, so Tyler did too. Tyler always had a way of aligning with his brothers.

Hygiene: The Battlefield

For years, hygiene was a battlefield.

On bath nights, the house moved like choreography. Jacob hopped in first, dunking plastic dinosaurs and narrating sea battles. I turned the water off before Tyler's toe touched the tile, silence first, always. He edged in heel-to-toe, testing the temperature with a fingertip before surrendering his weight. While Jacob splashed, Tyler lined foam letters along the porcelain ledge with surgeon precision: TV-PG, NICK JR., NICK AT NITE, rating logos from the corner of the screen, rebuilt from memory like spells to keep panic away.

No bubbles. No scents. No running water. Even then, he wouldn't go in alone. He needed Jacob.

We thought it was a quirk. We didn't understand yet: he wasn't avoiding language; he was hunting patterns, angles of a G, the straight back of a K, geometry he could trust in a world that was too loud and too loose.

The War Zone

Showers weren't disliked; they were panic. The bathroom became a war zone. He'd plant himself in the hall, arms locked, jaw set, as if the tub held fire. We rarely had to do showers in the younger years, but sometimes we found ourselves in a hotel or home with no tub for too many nights to skip baths.

The sound of the shower wasn't just noise to him; it was assault. A thin, needling hiss that filled every inch of the room, each droplet a strobe against his skin. He'd cover his ears and gasp, body trembling before the first drop even touched him. I used to watch his face twist in confusion and pain, and every instinct in me wanted to make it stop, turn off the water, scoop him up, and whisper apologies until it faded.

Sometimes, when I shut the door to muffle his screams, I'd press my forehead to the wood and wonder if I'd already broken him or if the world had. The line between cruelty and persistence blurred in that steam-fogged air. I hated how often I had to cross it. Some nights, I'd end up soaked, sitting on the bathroom floor with both of us anxious and overwhelmed, the air thick with shampoo and defeat. Love didn't always look like gentleness; sometimes it looked like staying when every part of you wanted to flee the sound.

I begged, bribed, bargained, threatened, cried. Some nights I sat on the floor outside the shower door, tears sliding down my face, trying to convince the water to stop being water.

The Sensory House

Our house in those years looked like a sensory therapy center. Weighted blankets folded neatly in baskets. Chew necklaces dangled from hooks by the door. Visual schedules taped to walls like artwork.

The little blue trampoline was a permanent fixture, placed right in the hall so Tyler could run to it whenever he needed. There were bins of fidget toys, noise-canceling headphones, and bins of identical socks because even the wrong texture could ruin a day.

I didn't know it then, but I was building a world where he could feel safe. What looked like clutter to outsiders was survival gear. Every object had a purpose: the heavy weight of the blanket that grounded him when storms brewed, the hum of the white noise machine that drowned out barking dogs and distant lawnmowers, the faint citrus smell of cleaning wipes; my attempt to scrub away the chaos I couldn't control.

SportsCenter Sanctuary

The television became another lifeline. Not cartoons. Not kids' shows. ESPN2.

He memorized the cadence of the announcers' voices, the exact order of highlights, and even the rhythm of the scrolling ticker at the bottom of the screen. Sports weren't entertainment; they were regulation. Predictable. Safe. ESPN2 was his sanctuary.

ESPN Birthday

Birthdays used to terrify me and Tyler as well. They were too loud, too unpredictable, too full of expectation. Every party felt like a gamble: Would he scream at the noise? Would the candles be too bright? I had learned to brace for chaos, even in celebration.

The year he asked for "ESPN" for his birthday, I thought he meant a jersey or a football-shaped cake. He didn't. He meant ESPN itself, the cadence, the graphics, the certainty of the ticker rolling bottom-screen like a heartbeat he could count on.

Nana took the idea and ran with it the way only she could. She found a baker willing to print the ESPN logo in red across a sheet cake and tracked down black-and-red streamers, foam fingers, and a banner that said "Welcome to SportsCenter" in letters cut from shiny cardstock. We moved her coffee table to the wall and propped her flat screen on a TV stand like a studio desk. She even printed tiny "lower thirds" with Tyler's name on them and taped one to a toy microphone.

The moment we carried him in, he froze. His eyes went wide, scanning the room: banner, streamers, the TV already tuned to ESPN2, Nana standing behind the "desk" and pretending to shuffle papers like an anchor. His lips parted. Then he beamed; a rare, full-face, unguarded smile that cracked me open.

"ESPN," he whispered reverently.

A cousin leaned over, confused. "Wait… is this like a sports theme?"

"It is sports," I said, a little too defensively. "It's his favorite thing."

Nana tapped the toy mic on the table. "We're live," she announced, and handed it to Tyler. He took it with both hands like it was made of glass. Jacob slid into frame beside him and shouted, "Breaking news! It's Tyler's birthday!" while Thomas pretended to run a camera with an empty paper towel roll. The room erupted in laughter.

When it was time for cake, the baker's glossy red ESPN logo stared up at him like a dream printed in sugar. He hovered his hand just over it, not touching, just seeing. Nana leaned in. "Ready for highlights?" she teased. He nodded hard, curls bouncing.

We sang. He didn't cover his ears this time. He didn't run. He stared at the cake, rocking gently, and when the last note fell, he whispered, "Again." We sang twice. (This is the last time we would sing happy birthday to him. Even now at 20 he will run off and hide from the singing of it for anyone's special day. He will acknowledge the occasion with a "Nappy Birthday" Facebook post and ask for it to remain level zero.)

A well-meaning guest murmured, "Someday he'll want a normal theme." I didn't flinch. This was normal for him. And watching his hands steady on that microphone, the ticker scrolling in the background like a lullaby, I realized that "normal" had no business defining our joy.

Later, when everyone left and the banner drooped, he sat on the floor, one hand on the toy mic, the other tracing the leftover frosting on the cake board. "ESPN birthday," he said to no one in particular, as if stamping it into memory. I wiped the counter and whispered back, "Yeah, baby. ESPN birthday." It was perfect because it was his.

Even now, Tyler dreams of becoming a sports broadcaster. At family holidays, we hold silly "Olympics" for the kids: egg races, water balloon tosses, and three-legged sprints. Tyler doesn't play; he grabs a microphone and narrates, steady and confident, the one in control while his siblings compete. He's found his lane, even in the noise. When he goes to our neighborhood events, he proudly takes his microphone and does interviews and highlights. In today's world, I have to smile because he is met with understanding, patience, and love as he interviews our neighbors and friends.

Where Is My Hairbrush?

His brothers and sisters didn't always understand. Jacob, especially, would get frustrated when Tyler insisted on routines or wouldn't play the way other kids did. But then there were moments when Jacob would step in without being asked, grabbing a juice box for Tyler before a meltdown, handing him the remote so ESPN2 could play again. Those flashes of sibling connection were rare gold in those days.

It started as a joke, born out of frustration when I couldn't find a single hairbrush in a house full of kids. But it didn't stay just mine; it became everyone's.

I'd call from the hallway:

"Oh, where is my hairbrush? Oh, where, oh where, oh where is my hairbrush?"

From the living room, Jacob would answer in a mock-serious voice:

"Mom, I think Thomas hid it!"

From the bathroom, Thomas would chime in, off-key but loud:

"Nooooo, Tyler took it!"

And then, like clockwork, Tyler's voice would ring out, sing-song, clear, echoing the melody I'd started:

"Oh, where is my hairbrush?"

The whole house would dissolve into laughter. It didn't matter that dinner was burning on the stove or that the laundry sat unfolded. For those few silly minutes, chaos turned into a chorus.

Sometimes, on the hardest days when therapy had wrung us all out, or when meltdowns left me on the bathroom floor, I'd start the song just to see if he'd answer. Every time he did, my shoulders dropped a little. It was proof that we could still reach each other, not with drills or charts, but with a ridiculous tune about a missing hairbrush.

Even now, decades later, I'll belt it out at the top of my lungs without warning. Tyler, twenty years old and taller than me, will still answer in that sing-song voice. And just like that, I'm back in the jumping years, surrounded by little voices shouting across the house, turning exhaustion into music. When the house is quiet and grown, I can still hear it; those overlapping voices echoing down a hallway that no longer exists. The rhythm of our chaos turned into a lullaby.

Reflection

Looking back, those years were loud, rigid, exhausting, and often lonely. People on the outside saw a quirky boy who bounced too much, loved broccoli, and recited sports stats like a pro. They didn't see the scaffolding holding him up, the endless therapy appointments, sleepless nights, and a family rearranging itself daily to meet his needs.

But I saw it. I lived it. And now, I see the gift buried in it all.

Because love didn't always look like hugs or "I love you." Sometimes it looked like broccoli jokes and trampoline marathons. Sometimes it sounded like ESPN commentary at a family Easter Olympics. Sometimes it hummed softly in a silly hairbrush song.

I now see that the jumping years weren't just about bouncing, or broccoli, or spaghetti sauce, or hairbrush songs. They were about survival. Not just his but mine too.

Jumping gave Tyler a way to keep his body from flying apart. Broccoli gave him something steady when the world shifted too fast. ESPN gave him rhythm and predictability when everything else felt like noise. And that ridiculous hairbrush song gave us laughter when we were both too tired to fight.

Each of those things became anchors. Small, strange, ordinary anchors. To an outsider, they looked like quirks, obsessions, even inconveniences. But to me, they were proof that he was finding ways to live in a world that didn't make sense to him and that I was learning to follow his lead instead of dragging him along.

His siblings were part of that survival too. Jacob handing him the remote without being asked. Thomas echoing his words until they became a chorus. Justin toddling behind, adapting before he even knew what adaptation meant. Hailey watching cartoons with him. They all learned early that love doesn't always look like hugs or bedtime stories. Sometimes it looks like strained tomato sauce, stocked broccoli, and a trampoline in the middle of the living room.

And I learned that too.

I used to think love had to be big. A breakthrough, a milestone, a miracle moment. But the jumping years taught me the truth: love is in the persistence. Love is in the rhythm. Love is in the way we show up, again and again, no matter how strange the rituals might look from the outside. Somewhere along the way, I stopped trying to fix the noise and started listening to it. The rhythm that once felt like chaos became our language. I found my calm inside his motion.

The jumping years were exhausting. They were messy. They were lonely. But they were also unforgettable. Because every bounce, every chant of "jump, jump, jump," every broccoli joke, every ESPN birthday, every silly hairbrush duet was Tyler's way of saying:

I'm here. This is who I am. Will you meet me here?

And the answer, always, was yes.

Escapes and Expansions

Grief Folds Time

Grief has a way of folding time. Some days I remember with perfect clarity, every detail sharp and bright. Others feel erased, like I was living underwater.

This is one I will never forget.

I went in for a routine checkup, excited to hear the sound I loved most: the rhythmic thump of my baby's heartbeat. We were sure she was our first little girl. I'd felt her kick. I'd imagined bows and dresses. I'd already started picturing her future.

The Four Days of Waiting

The doctor's expression shifted. He pulled out the bigger machine, the one that made me nervous just by its size. His silence said more than words ever could.

I left that appointment with news no mother should ever have to carry: the baby I loved, the one I'd been dreaming of, was gone.

For reasons I'll never fully understand, they made me wait four days before I could go to the hospital to be induced. Four days carrying a lifeless baby inside me. Four days smiling for Tyler and his siblings, holding his routine together, telling the kids Tee Tee and Pop Pop would be coming to stay because "Mommy's going to send the baby to heaven."

Four days pretending I wasn't falling apart.

Each day felt stolen.

The house looked the same, therapy charts taped to the fridge, the scent of laundry detergent still clinging to Tyler's weighted blanket, but the air felt wrong. I kept catching myself reaching for my stomach, waiting for a kick that never came.

Morning routines blurred into survival. Tyler's voice still filled the kitchen, asking for the same cereal, the same spoon, and the same show. I remember watching him bounce in front of the TV while I stirred oatmeal that no one really ate, pretending that the world was normal.

Every night, I sat on the bathroom floor and folded tiny onesies that would never be worn. I couldn't stop myself. My body was still in mother mode, counting, washing, preparing, even though my heart already knew the ending.

The hardest part was pretending. Pretending for the boys, for Dad, for the neighbors who asked if I was "so excited." I nodded and smiled and lied with a voice that wasn't mine. At night, I'd lay in bed, hand on my belly, whispering apologies into the dark.

I told myself that if I could keep Tyler's routine intact, maybe everything else would stay intact too.

Breakfast. Therapy. Bath. Trampoline. Dinner. Bed. Repeat.

It was the only rhythm that made sense anymore.

On the third night, when the house was finally quiet, I slipped outside. The stars were sharp and endless. I remember looking up and wondering if she was already among them. My breath made clouds in the cold air. Somewhere inside, I could hear Tyler humming to himself the same three-note tune he always sang when he felt calm. That small sound anchored me to the earth.

The world hadn't stopped after all. I was still here. He was still here.

That had to be enough.

"I went through those days in fragments: one breath, one fake smile, one routine at a time. Tyler's laughter was the only sound that didn't feel like it belonged in a dream."

Delivering Silence

When the day came, I walked into Labor and Delivery with a tiny mound under my shirt, too far along for a D&C, not far enough to save her. I would have to deliver her lifeless, warm, but gone. The lady at the desk argued I needed the ER, assuming I was some young, dumb mom who came to labor and delivery with such a tiny bump. The loss was bad enough without having to apologize and explain I was there to deliver a baby no matter how small I was, or how she made me feel.

The hospital smelled like antiseptic and lemon cleaner, that sharp scent that stings your nose and makes you feel smaller somehow. The nurse spoke softly, too softly, like her words might shatter. I remember staring at the white tile floor, at the scuff marks from a thousand gurneys before mine and thinking how strange it was that grief had a smell, a color, a sound.

They would induce me. I would go through labor. And I would deliver a baby I'd never hear cry. A baby I'd never hold to my chest or hear call me "Mommy." A baby that would never grow larger than the palm of my hand but would live forever in my heart.

When the IV slid in, the metal was cold against my skin. Every beep of the monitor was a countdown. I focused on the rhythm, trying to find comfort in the mechanical predictability of it. At least something in the room had order.

There was no panic, no rush of nurses shouting commands, just quiet professionalism and a kind of mercy I didn't know how to receive. The contractions came, sharp and fast, my body moving through a process that had no purpose anymore.

I remember watching the clock. Hours, minutes, seconds, none of it mattered. The world had stopped.

And then the silence came.

Not the comfortable kind. The kind that presses on your chest until you can't breathe. The kind that feels like the air itself is mourning with you.

Somewhere in the hallway, another mother's baby cried thinly, wailing, alive. That sound carved straight through me.

When it was over, the doctor asked if I wanted to hold her. I couldn't. I wanted to, but my hands wouldn't move. I just nodded, and she placed that impossibly small bundle beside me for one brief, eternal moment.

There are no words for holding someone who never had the chance to hold you.

And that wasn't even the worst of it.

The Second Battle: My Own Life

A week later, I found myself in the hospital again, this time fighting for my life.

I'd been sent home with a retained placenta, something I'd tried to tell my doctors about but wasn't believed. "Rest," they said. "You just need time." So I rested. I trusted them. They insisted nothing was wrong and that I was just grieving.

Seven days passed, and I drove three hours away to try on dresses for my sister's wedding. That night, I collapsed.

I remember being in the hotel bathroom, freezing and weak, while Dad, my sister, and her fiancé sat in the next room eating dinner. I remember the world tilting. I remember darkness. And then, I remember a field of magnolias. The tile was cold beneath me, smooth, slick, and merciless. The bathroom light flickered, casting long shadows that made the walls breathe. I tried to call out, but my voice sounded far away, swallowed by the sound of running water and the faint hum of the hotel's air vent.

My fingers slipped against the counter as I tried to stand. The world tilted. My reflection in the mirror blurred into streaks of white and red. I could hear my dad laughing faintly from the other room, my sister's voice, silverware clinking against a table, ordinary sounds that suddenly felt like echoes from another life.

Then the cold gave way to warmth. Sunlight, golden and endless.

The field of magnolias unfolded around me, each petal brighter than snow, soft as silk against my fingertips. The air smelled sweet, the way spring mornings did when life was still simple.

And she was there. The blonde girl.

She wasn't a ghost; she was light. Gentle, curious, waiting.

When I stepped toward her, the world vibrated like a string pulled too tight.

"Not yet," she whispered, though her lips never moved.

I believe now that the girl was Hailey, choosing me as her mom before she was even conceived. She was born that December.

Somewhere in the haze of unconsciousness and that field of magnolias, I heard my nephew crying in the next room; he was the same age as my youngest son, and in that state, I thought it was my son, Justin, crying for me. As any mother would, I found the strength to wake up and try to get to him. My nephew saved my life that night.

Dad had to slap me repeatedly to keep me awake until the ambulance arrived. Chaos swirled around me, paramedics rushing, doctors yelling, forms being signed for blood transfusions. I was in hemorrhagic shock. They barely saved me in time. They estimated a loss of 6 to 7 units of blood. Unheard of, they said. I wouldn't make it through the evening.

I drifted in and out, floating between pain and light, until finally, there was the sterile brightness of the hospital ceiling and the quiet relief of survival.

When I woke up hours later, I was surrounded by machines and faces streaked with tears. I couldn't speak. I just whispered, "I'm still here."

And somehow, I was.

The World Rebuilds

I came home alive. I went on to have more children. But those weeks were the hardest of my life. I felt fragile, hollow, and terrified.

And yet, I didn't have the luxury of falling apart. Every morning, I packed therapy bags, cut crusts off sandwiches, and drove the same routes, pretending the world hadn't cracked open. Tyler didn't know how close he'd come to losing me, but in his way, he saved me; the rhythm of his needs tethered me to the living.

There were therapy schedules taped to the fridge. Tyler's life revolved around routine, and I had to keep it steady for him even when my own life was shaking. There were meals to cook, baths to give, and meltdowns to soothe. Grief and exhaustion hung over me like a storm cloud, but I couldn't let it rain on my kids.

I smiled when I had nothing left. I kept moving when I wanted to disappear. Because they needed me.

But I needed something, too. Something to hold on to. Something to make me feel alive again.

World of Warcraft: Our Second Language

That's when we found World of Warcraft.

It started as a distraction. Something to fill the silence once the kids were asleep, when the house felt too big and my thoughts too loud. The glow of the computer was a comforting, small, steady light in the dark.

The first time the music played, I remember freezing. It was soft, orchestral, almost holy. It didn't sound like a game. It sounded like possibility.

Dad sat beside me, explaining how to move, how to fight, how to live in this new world. And for a few minutes, grief loosened its grip.

Then Jacob joined us. He was quick, clever, and already strategizing like a commander. Tyler leaned against my shoulder, eyes wide, completely still, the kind of stillness that meant he was memorizing everything.

When he finally took the mouse, something clicked literally and figuratively. He didn't hesitate. He understood instinctively. Where to go, what to do, and what each button meant. It was as if the rules of this digital world were written in his language.

The house filled with a new kind of sound: the rhythmic click of keyboards, the soft hum of the fan, our laughter echoing off the walls. Sometimes the kids fell asleep mid-quest, heads resting on folded arms, screens glowing blue across their faces.

I started to notice something else, too: Tyler was more confident here. More open. He gave directions, made decisions, and even comforted us when things went wrong.

When he said "Follow me," we did.

There was a night when the power flickered mid-battle, and the whole house groaned. "No!" Tyler yelled, hands frozen mid-air. But when the lights came back on, he laughed a big, full-body laughter that shook the chair.

It wasn't just a game anymore. It was our home inside a home, a space where grief didn't reach us.

The Language of Joy

The game became a family language. We'd gather at the kitchen table, laptops lined up, shouting directions at each other as we played. Laughter filled the house in a way I hadn't heard in months after losing the baby. We would even splurge on pizza or hoagies and just have a night or weekend where our only reality was the one we created together. Where everyone was the same and Tyler was the hero of our story.

Sometimes we'd all fail spectacularly, and Tyler would laugh so hard he'd fall over in his chair. Other nights, we'd pull off impossible victories and cheer like we'd just won the lottery. One night, Jacob spilled soda across the keyboard mid-fight. Thomas was yelling "heal me!" and Tyler, unbothered, calmly said, "We're doomed." Then he cracked up laughing so hard he fell backward in his chair.

I can still hear that deep, uncontrollable laughter that comes from pure joy, not from jokes or comedy, but from belonging.

I remember looking around the room: mismatched laptops on the table, pizza boxes stacked like trophies, the air warm with the hum of electronics and family. For a second, I thought this was what healing sounds like. Not therapy, not progress notes. Just laughter.

And through it all, Tyler thrived.

In real life, he struggled to join conversations, to find his footing in a noisy, unpredictable world. But in this world, he was confident. Capable. Strategic. People respected him for his skill, not because they were told to be "patient" with him.

It was a glimpse into the boy I always knew was there.

The graphics have evolved; the game has changed, and so have we. Even our family dynamic has changed. We added Hailey, then Dad and Mom divorced. Now it is Mom and Kris; we have bonus siblings and baby sisters. But that virtual world has been a constant through deployments, divorces, heartbreaks, therapy marathons, life changes, and victories big and small.

The Hero at the Front Lines

Thomas started playing too, and one time he and I were on a mission for a mount. We tried and failed before asking Jacob to join; again, we tried and failed. Finally, we got Tyler to come along.

"Wait for me," he said, his voice steady. "I've got it."

He took control, perfectly timing his abilities, giving Jacob the space to heal, guiding us through the fight like a seasoned leader. When we won, he leaned back with a grin.

"Saved us," he said simply.

And he had.

Those nights gave me something I didn't know I needed.

They gave me a way to connect with Tyler beyond therapy drills and picture cards. They gave him confidence and independence. And they gave me a way to escape grief, not to ignore it, but to catch my breath from it.

In World of Warcraft, Tyler wasn't "the boy with autism." He wasn't a list of deficits on a report. He wasn't underestimated. He was a hero in epic armor, a leader people trusted. We were a family of the Alliance working together to save Azeroth from doom.

For a few hours a night, I wasn't a mother drowning in trauma and responsibilities; I was just a mage defending an alliance of honor.

Even as the years passed, the game stayed a part of us. For a few years, even Hailey and Justin took over our accounts, laughing as they explored the world with us. Now, Lynnlee is learning to slay dragons too, when she's not busy having adventures with Harper and inspiring Hugsy's stories.

What Endures

For Tyler, it's still a sanctuary. He knows every inch of Azeroth, every dungeon mechanic, every lore detail. He's a leader in that world, and I love watching him in his element, commanding a room full of strangers with calm authority.

For me, it's a reminder of survival.

People talk about milestones, diagnoses, and therapies. They rarely talk about joy. They rarely talk about the unexpected places where we find connection.

World of Warcraft is more than a game to me. It's proof that Tyler's world is vast and magical, even if people can't always see it. It's proof that healing doesn't always come in a doctor's office or therapy room. Sometimes it comes at a kitchen table, under the glow of a computer screen, with your kids laughing beside you.

It's proof that even in grief, there's still adventure.

I'll never forget the night Tyler leaned over after a dungeon run, his face lit up by the screen, and said, "we're a good team."

And we were. We still are. Although these days he rolls his eyes at me playing retail and he just wants to play classic, but when I really need him, he never fails to hop over and slay a dragon, or some other source of evil just to make me smile (okay, maybe it's to make me leave him alone, but let me have this moment).

We've saved worlds together in that game. But really, World of Warcraft saved us.

It gave me an escape when grief nearly crushed me. It gave Tyler a voice and a world where he wasn't labeled. It gave our family a space to laugh when laughter felt impossible.

Together, we are not just a mom and her son navigating a hard world.

We're heroes on a mission.

Sometimes, when I pass Tyler's room late at night, I see the glow of his monitor through the door crack. I hear the faint sound of the game's theme music, that familiar melody that once saved us both.

He's older now, quieter, more confident. But when he turns and grins, it's the same look he had when he was ten and shouted, "We won!"

There's a stack of binders in the attic that once defined his worth. And there's a digital world downstairs that redefined it.

I used to think healing came from fixing what was broken.

Now I know it comes from playing anyway.

The Binder

It wasn't a baby book.

It wasn't a scrapbook.

It wasn't even a diary.

It was a three-inch, three-ring beast of plastic and paper.

It smelled faintly of ink and coffee; motherhood turned into paperwork. The plastic cover was always cool to the touch, slick under my palm, like the hospital binder they handed me the day he was born.

The Birth of the Binder

I didn't start The Binder because I wanted to; I started it because I didn't know what else to do.

For most of his life, I was documenting, journaling, and researching. I had folder upon folder of theories, research, Dr. notes, school notes, milestones, and memories.

The night after Tyler's first developmental evaluation, I sat at the kitchen table under the harsh light of a single bulb, surrounded by crumpled appointment cards and handouts. The house was finally quiet, but my mind wasn't. The air still carried the faint tang of disinfectant from the clinic, and my hands smelled like the soap from the hospital bathroom where I'd cried before driving home.

They had given me a manila folder that felt heavier than it should have. Inside: intake forms, goals, "parent strategies," and one typed page that began, Areas of Concern. That phrase hit me harder than any diagnosis ever could. I ran my fingers over the bold letters, as if touch alone could soften them.

There was no instruction manual for autism, no roadmap for what came next, just this stack of papers that somehow held my son's future. So I found a binder.

It wasn't even new; it was one of Jacob's old school binders, the kind with doodles in Sharpie across the front. I dumped his spelling worksheets out and wiped it clean with a Clorox wipe, the ink bleeding just enough to stain my fingers blue. Then I hole-punched every page and began to sort.

Intake. Speech. Occupational therapy. Insurance. Each tab is a new kind of grief.

Tyler slept on the couch behind me, his arm draped over a plastic dinosaur, the blue light from the muted TV flickering across his face. Every few minutes he'd make a little humming sound, the same one he made when he was content. I remember thinking how unfair it was that a word like autism could sound so heavy in an office and yet look so peaceful in my living room.

By the time I finished, the binder was thick enough that it barely closed. I snapped the rings shut, the sound echoing through the kitchen like a gavel.

That was the moment I understood what this thing really was, not just paperwork, but a shield. I didn't know yet what battles I'd be fighting, only that they were coming.

When I slipped the binder onto the counter beside the coffee maker, I caught a glimpse of my reflection in the microwave door: tired eyes, shoulders rounded forward, a mother holding a new kind of baby.

That binder grew with him. Every new appointment, every evaluation, every progress report was another page. I stopped decorating walls with family photos because I couldn't stand to see the contrast: life captured in smiles beside life reduced to data.

Still, I kept it organized, polished, ready. I didn't know it then, but I was building the language of defense, alphabetized love, and laminated resilience.

If Tyler had a biography before he could speak, this was it. Page after page, tab after tab, diagnosis after diagnosis. Coffee stains on the cover, chewed-up corners from being shoved into bags, Post-its hanging like flags of surrender. It weighed more than he did the day he was born, and sometimes it felt like it carried us both.

The Language of Deficit

Inside were acronyms that could have been their own language: IEP, ARD, OT, ABA, FAPE, LRE. Entire lifetimes of red tape condensed into letter soup. Each page was a snapshot of someone else's version of my son. None of them were mine.

"Tyler demonstrates maladaptive self-regulation."

Translation: He cries when overwhelmed.

"Limited eye contact, perseverative language."

Translation: He repeats things he loves until you want to scream, and it's the most joyful sound in my house.

Repetitive language and interests. Translation: He can recite every ESPN2 anchor since 2003, and somehow, it's beautiful.

The first time I opened it, that word, deficit, jumped out in bold. I sat at the kitchen table, coffee gone cold, staring at it like it was a personal insult instead of a clinical term.

The binder never recorded the way he lined up cars with precision; his brows knit together in concentration most adults could only fake. It never logged how his whole face lit up when he heard the ESPN2 theme song. No report ever captured the way he pressed his forehead to mine when words failed him, but love didn't.

The Binder wasn't made for that. The Binder was made for deficits.

The language inside The Binder was its own dialect: cold, concise, and completely detached from love. Every page spoke in code. I used to joke that I needed a decoder ring just to understand my own child.

The first time I read one of Tyler's occupational therapy evaluations, I had to stop halfway through because my throat burned. The words were clean and clinical, like they'd been scrubbed of anything human. "Demonstrates poor fine motor planning." "Limited proprioceptive awareness." "Requires hand-over-hand assistance for multi-step tasks."

That last one stuck with me.

I looked up from the paper to where he was sitting in the living room, methodically lining up his toy cars: red, blue, green, red, blue, green, and thought, How can anyone call that poor planning?

I didn't understand how someone could watch him do that, see that perfect pattern, and decide the conclusion was "deficit."

Then came the speech evaluation. Three pages in, I stopped counting the number of times the word "limited" appeared. Limited eye contact. Limited spontaneous language. Limited social reciprocity.

But what they never wrote, what I saw every day, was that Tyler's limited words were chosen with infinite precision. He didn't waste them. If he said "juice," he meant it. If he said "no," he meant that, too. I used to think maybe the rest of us were the ones who overused language, flooding the world with noise while he focused on truth.

Late at night, after the kids were asleep, I'd sit at the kitchen table flipping through pages under the yellow light of the stove hood, a cup of coffee gone cold beside me. The words started to blur together after a while. I could almost hear the rhythm of them, that sterile heartbeat of professional detachment: observed... assessed... noted... recommended.

Sometimes I'd read a line and laugh because it sounded so absurd aloud.

"Tyler demonstrates inappropriate play behaviors."

Translation: He drives toy cars across the couch instead of on the floor.

"Displays rigid thinking patterns."

Translation: He knows exactly what he wants and refuses to settle for less, same as every man in this family.

I started writing my own translations in the margins with a red pen. It was my quiet rebellion.

"Maladaptive coping strategies," one report reads.

I wrote underneath: Loves his trampoline, same as I love coffee. Survival method, not a malfunction.

There was one report that gutted me. It was short, just three sentences.

"Tyler demonstrates little interest in peer interaction. Does not engage in reciprocal play."

That line lived in my chest for weeks. It made him sound unreachable, untouchable. But at home, Jacob would crawl beside him, both boys pushing toy trains around the floor in silence, perfectly content. I used to watch them and think, This looks pretty reciprocal to me.

The longer The Binder grew, the less I recognized my son inside it. Each new report seemed to overwrite the last, layering on jargon until the boy I knew disappeared behind words like adaptive function and goal acquisition rate.

I began to notice how the language crept into my own. I'd catch myself talking like them at appointments, "He's displaying sensory-seeking behavior today" instead of "He's climbing the counter again." Somewhere along the way, motherhood had become a professional role I never applied for.

I started keeping a notebook tucked in the back pocket of The Binder as my own counter-documentation. While the official pages said "deficit," mine said things like:

- Laughed for five full minutes when the cat sneezed.
- Memorized every word to the Cars movie.
- Learned to unzip his hoodie without help.
- Let me brush his hair without crying.

Tiny miracles. The kind that didn't earn data points but kept us both alive.

Some days, after therapy, I'd pull the binder out of my bag in the car and just hold it against my chest, its edges digging into my arms. It was heavy, but what made it unbearable wasn't the weight of paper. It was the feeling that every page had already decided who he was allowed to be.

I learned to carry it like a weapon.

IEP meeting? Slam it on the table and watch the ripple move across the room. Administrators straightened their backs. Teachers shuffled their notes. Because The Binder meant I wasn't just another "emotional mom." I had documentation, data, signatures, timelines. They might dismiss me, but they couldn't dismiss several pounds of proof.

The Meeting

The first time I ever walked into an IEP meeting, I was naïve enough to think it was a conversation. I didn't realize it was a negotiation disguised as collaboration.

Back then, I carried my binder like a child carries a backpack, too big for me, awkward, and clumsy. I thought they were the experts. They had clipboards and degrees. I had instinct and heart. I didn't know that instinct would become the sharpest weapon I'd ever wield.

Years later, by the time of the meeting, I was different. I'd learned their language. I'd learned how to underline and highlight strategically, how to quote page numbers, and how to keep my voice steady even when I wanted to scream.

That morning, I packed my bag the way a soldier packs gear before battle: highlighters, sticky notes, copies of every report, a travel mug of coffee so strong it could peel paint. I slipped on my cardigan, the "respectable mom armor," and stared in the mirror before leaving. I looked calm. But I could already feel my pulse in my teeth.

This meeting is seared into me like a scar: that institutional tang of public schools. A long table, too many chairs. Six staff members, one of me. Tyler's whole year was about to be reduced to a vote. The fluorescent lights hummed. The smell of burnt coffee clung to the air, mixed with the sharp tang of Expo markers. Someone had sprayed perfume that gave me a headache. I straightened my stack of papers, armor disguised as stationery.

I lugged The Binder in and let it drop on the table with a satisfying thud. The sound startled the speech therapist. Good.

They started with pleasantries, but we all knew what this was. They wanted to reduce his services. The school gets more funding if they "mainstream" my son. As if they miraculously cured him of something that we came to learn needed no cure. He was not broken; he was just different than they were.

"Based on our recent evaluations," one administrator began, sliding a packet toward me, "we don't feel Tyler qualifies for extended one-on-one support. His progress shows he can function in a group setting with minimal assistance."

Heat rose in my chest, but I kept my voice steady. I flipped to the tab highlighted in neon yellow. "That's interesting," I said, "because on September 14th, his occupational therapist wrote…" I ran my finger down the page until I found the line. "'Requires full physical prompts to initiate handwriting tasks. Cannot independently grasp a pencil.'"

I looked up. "So tell me again how he can function in a group setting? Because unless that group includes someone holding the pencil for him, I don't see how this makes sense."

Silence. The special ed coordinator cleared her throat. The speech therapist scribbled something down.

I pressed harder. "Or maybe you'd like me to read from his ABA evaluation? Page 127, tab three. It says, 'Tyler demonstrates extreme distress when separated from adult support in structured activities.' That's not minimal assistance. That's survival."

The principal shifted in her chair. "Ms. Hinkle, we do recognize Tyler's needs."

I snapped the binder shut, the sound echoing off the cinderblock walls. "No. You recognize budget cuts. You recognize staffing shortages. But don't sit here and tell me my son doesn't qualify when your own words say otherwise."

The room went still. Finally, one teacher spoke, soft but steady. "She's right. He does struggle more than what is written here."

For a split second, I wanted to cry, not from anger, but from relief that someone else finally saw him the way I did.

The meeting dragged on for another hour. They promised to "review the data." I promised to keep showing up.

When it ended, I walked out clutching the binder to my chest. My shoulders were tight, my legs shaky. The hallway smelled faintly of crayons and floor wax, that strange mix of innocence and bureaucracy.

Outside, the sunlight hit me so hard I had to squint. The air felt too open after the stale room. I stood by my car for a minute, binder pressed against me like armor, watching kids run on the playground. Their laughter carried across the parking lot, pure, wild, unmeasured.

That's what I wanted for Tyler. Not independence measured in percentages or charts. Just laughter.

When I got home, I laid the binder on the counter and poured a cup of coffee I didn't drink. My hand still hurt from gripping it so tightly.

That night, I wrote a note in the back pocket.

Remember: they are trained to talk in data. You are trained to talk in love. Don't let them confuse the two.

And yet, the binder haunted me.

It wasn't just paper; it was a mirror of how the world saw my child. Cold, clinical, detached. Every page was a deficit; every sentence a shortfall.

The pages I hated most weren't the brutal evaluations. It was the progress notes.

"Tyler tolerated brushing his teeth with minimal distress today."

Progress? Maybe. But at home, I knew he was still swallowing his baby teeth whole because he was terrified of letting them fall out. That wasn't in the binder. It never would be.

The Missing Page

The first time I lost a page, it wasn't just paper. It was oxygen leaving the room.

It started small: an empty tab. I had the binder open across the living room floor, color-coded tabs fanned out like a deck of cards. The TV hummed quietly in the background, some late-night news show I wasn't really watching. The kids had gone to bed hours ago. Tyler's rhythmic hum floated faintly from his room down the hall; steady and predictable, the sound of him winding down.

When I flipped to the Speech section and saw the gap, my heart kicked hard against my ribs. One evaluation was missing. Just one. But in that moment, it felt like the foundation had cracked.

I checked again. Front to back. Each tab was lifted carefully. Nothing.

Then came the second wave: the adrenaline. That awful, heavy heat in the chest that feels like panic and guilt braided together.

The living room became a war zone. Couch cushions on the floor. Diaper bag dumped out. Crayons rolling across the tile. I tore open drawers, checked under furniture, and even looked in the freezer once because panic doesn't make sense.

At one point, I found myself kneeling by the trash can, flipping through greasy paper towels and half-eaten chicken nuggets. My hands smelled like ketchup and paper ink. I didn't care.

"Where is it?" I muttered aloud, my voice sharp in the empty room.

Every few minutes I'd stop and listen to the refrigerator hum, to Tyler's distant breathing, to the click of the ceiling fan. And every sound felt too loud, like the world was taunting me with its normalcy while mine unraveled over a missing sheet of paper.

By midnight, the house looked like evidence of a crime I couldn't explain. Paper piles towered on the couch. Sticky notes clung to my socks. Even the dog avoided the living room.

Jacob peeked out from the hallway, his hair messy with sleep. "Mom? What are you doing?"

I froze. My throat tightened.

"Looking for something important," I said.

He yawned, rubbed his eyes, and disappeared again. A moment later, I heard him whisper to one of his brothers, "She's looking for Tyler."

I almost laughed, but it came out broken. Because that's exactly what it felt like. Like if I didn't find that page, some part of Tyler would vanish, erased, undocumented, unrecognized.

It sounds irrational now. But when you spend years having to prove your child exists in systems built on paperwork, even a missing signature feels like erasure.

At 1:00 a.m., I sat cross-legged in the middle of the floor, surrounded by chaos. The faint smell of coffee and paper mixed with something else: the iron scent of exhaustion. Tears came, hot and fast, falling onto the open binder. The pages rippled where they landed.

I whispered to no one, "You are not your paperwork."

It was half prayer, half protest.

By 2:00, I'd accepted defeat. I left everything spread out and crawled into bed beside Tyler. His curls tickled my chin. He shifted in his sleep and muttered something about "ESPN." I lay there, staring at the ceiling, feeling the silence thrum in my ears.

At dawn, I found it.

Folded in half, wedged between the car seat and the passenger door. Creased, dusty, but intact.

I sat there in the driveway holding it like a relic. The morning air was cool and smelled faintly of cut grass and gasoline. I smoothed the paper flat on my knee, tracing the creases with my thumb until the words came back into focus.

It wasn't even a groundbreaking evaluation. Just speech notes routine, redundant. But to me, it felt like finding him again.

When I slid it back into The Binder, the rings snapped shut with a satisfying click. For a long moment, I just held it against my chest. My heart slowed. My breath came back.

At the next meeting, no one even looked at that page.

But I did. And that was enough.

That night, I tucked the binder under my bed instead of the bookshelf. For months after, I couldn't sleep unless I knew it was within reach. As ridiculous as it sounds, that binder had become my security blanket, the one thing I could control in a life that felt ruled by unpredictability.

And every time I opened it, that page, the one that had almost disappeared, was the first thing I checked.

The Fire Fantasy

At night, when everyone was asleep, I'd stand in the kitchen. The Binder lay open on the counter, pages spread and tabs bent. The only sound was the faint hum of the refrigerator.

There was a strange comfort in the way it looked under the kitchen light. Familiar chaos turned into order with three metal rings. But there was also resentment.

That binder had followed me through five houses, countless schools, and a thousand tears. It sat in my passenger seat like a co-pilot I never chose. Every time I saw it, a quiet fury bubbled beneath the exhaustion.

That's when the fantasy began.

I'd picture myself dragging it out to the driveway, barefoot, the pavement still warm from the sun. The night would be quiet that thick, rural kind of quiet where even the crickets seem to pause when something sacred is about to happen.

In one hand, a Bic lighter. In the other, years of other people's opinions.

The first flick of the lighter would break the silence; that soft, percussive chhhk was followed by a blue flame that trembled like doubt. I could almost smell it: paper, ink, and the faint chemical sweetness of melting plastic.

The fire would start slowly.

One corner is catching. The page is curling inward, turning the word "deficit" into a dark line of ash. Acronyms are dissolving: IEP, ARD, FAPE, smoke ghosts rising toward the stars.

I'd feed it page by page.

"Maladaptive behavior" — gone.

"Requires redirection to complete tasks." — gone.

"Cognitive functioning below peer average." — gone.

The smoke would rise like a prayer I never knew how to say.

I imagined the neighbors seeing the glow from their windows and wondering what kind of mother burns paperwork at midnight. But maybe some things have to be burned to make space for what's real.

Because here's the truth:

I hated that binder.

I hated how it reduced him to checkboxes and data points. I hated how it had the power to decide what support he got, what programs he qualified for, and what future someone else thought he deserved.

But mostly, I hated what it did to me.

It turned me into someone constantly defending, constantly proving, constantly afraid that if I missed a meeting or lost a signature, the world would forget my child existed.

That's what the fire was really about. Not destruction but liberation.

In my mind, I could see the ashes swirling up into the night sky, tiny black feathers floating away. I imagined them scattering across the yard, drifting into the grass, mingling with the dirt and the scent of rain.

In the glow of that imagined fire, I saw Tyler, barefoot on the porch, hair wild, trampoline squeaking in the distance. He wasn't the words on those pages. He was laughter and motion and sound. He was alive.

Sometimes, I'd close my eyes and imagine the final moment when the last page, the cover itself, finally caught fire. The plastic would warp and shriek, and the word "Binder" would melt into something unreadable.

Smoke would cling to my clothes. The air would taste like closure.

But I never lit the match.

Because as much as I longed for freedom from it, I still needed it. The Binder wasn't just a burden; it was armor. The one thing that made them listen. The proof that love, when translated into data, could still be powerful.

So I didn't burn it.

Instead, I packed it into a storage tub and carried it up to the attic. The dust up there clung to my arms, the air heavy with insulation and memory. I placed it in the corner, away from the Christmas boxes, away from everything else its own quiet grave.

For a moment, I just stood there, staring at it in the dim yellow light. I thought about all the rooms I'd carried it into. All the tables I'd slammed it on. All the times it had made people take me seriously.

Then I whispered, "Rest."

And I closed the attic door.

Sometimes, when the house is quiet, I still think about it up there. The weight of it. The sound of its rings clicking shut. The smell of ink and old paper waiting for air.

And I know if I ever need it again, it's there. But it doesn't own me anymore.

What Remains

That night, after tucking everyone into bed, I sat on the edge of the couch with a mug of tea that had long since gone cold. The house was finally still, the kind of silence that buzzes in your ears after a long day.

Somewhere upstairs, I knew The Binder sat waiting, boxed and heavy, its weight pressed into the attic floor like a ghost that still wanted to be seen. But I didn't go to it. I didn't need to.

Instead, I let myself breathe.

For the first time in years, I didn't feel the need to check tabs or reread reports. I didn't need to highlight or prepare or prove. My hands were empty, and it felt strange, but in the best way.

A soft creak pulled me from my thoughts. Tyler's door cracked open, a sliver of hallway light spilling onto the carpet. He shuffled out, hair tousled and eyes half-closed.

"Can I sit with you, Mom?"

His voice was sleepy, small in that fragile space between boy and man.

"Of course," I said, lifting the blanket. He crawled up beside me, his head finding the same spot on my shoulder that it had found since he was four years old.

He smelled like apple shampoo and dryer sheets, that faint, warm scent that only belongs to your own children. His fingers traced small circles on my arm, rhythmic and grounding.

Neither of us spoke for a while. The only sound was the hum of the refrigerator and the steady tick of the kitchen clock, that same clock that had watched me panic, argue, fight, and love across so many years.

If I closed my eyes, I could almost see the ghosts of every version of us: me on the floor surrounded by papers, him bouncing on the trampoline, the two of us learning each other's language one sound at a time.

He broke the silence first.

"Mom, remember when the school said I couldn't do group work?"

I laughed softly. "I remember."

"Well," he said, half grinning, "I helped Lynnlee with her logic today. That's group work."

There it was, the thing no binder could ever measure. The way he redefined his own limits without ever realizing it.

I felt my throat tighten. "That's more than group work, baby. That's growth."

He didn't respond; he just smiled, satisfied, and settled deeper against me.

And in that moment, I realized something: The Binder may have told the world who they thought he was, but it was moments like this that told me who he really is.

The pages upstairs were filled with deficits, goals, and data points.

Here on this couch, the data was different: warmth, presence, laughter, breath.

For years, I believed advocacy was about fighting. About walking into rooms with binders and fire and facts. But advocacy is also the quiet proof of survival, the love that outlasts paperwork, the nights when you don't need to say anything at all.

Because in the end, what remains isn't the paperwork.

It's the person.

It's the sound of your son's heartbeat pressed against your shoulder while the world sleeps.

It's the way he still hums softly when he's content, the way his laughter fills a room and erases every acronym that ever tried to define him.

It's the way he says "Mom" steady, sure, without hesitation.

Someday, someone else will open The Binder again. Maybe a future employer, a caseworker, a therapist. They'll flip through those pages and see words like limited eye contact and perseverative behavior.

But I'll know better.

I'll remember the boy who spent hours calling fake baseball games with his brothers. The teenager who insists on broccoli for dinner because it's "the healthiest green." The young man who makes his baby sister laugh until she hiccups.

That's his real record.

And maybe someday, when I'm gone and someone cleans out the attic, they'll find that binder still heavy, still full of other people's words. Maybe they'll wonder why I never threw it away.

I hope they understand.

I didn't keep it because of what was written inside.

I kept it because of everything it couldn't hold.

Because love doesn't fit in plastic sleeves.

Because progress doesn't always show up on data charts.

Because sometimes the most important story is the one you write after the paperwork ends.

I brushed a hand through Tyler's curls and whispered, "You did it, kid. You proved them all wrong."

He didn't answer because he was already asleep.

The clock ticked on. The house breathed around us.

And somewhere above, in the attic, The Binder rested finally quiet, finally powerless.

Brothers and Sisters

The Bridge Between Worlds

I used to think Tyler's story was mine to tell. The sleepless nights, the appointments, the meltdowns, the breakthroughs. I was there for every single one of them. But somewhere along the way, I realized it wasn't a story that belonged to Tyler and me alone. It belonged to all of us. Every sibling, every child who grew up learning to orbit around their brother's world, learning what it meant to love him on his terms.

Because raising one child with autism doesn't happen in isolation, even if it felt like it. The whole family grows around it, our roots twisting together, bending, finding sunlight in strange directions. Love gets redistributed. Time gets rationed. Patience becomes currency. But something else happens too, something harder to see in the chaos. Compassion takes root early. Understanding blooms before most kids even know what that word means.

Each of my children learned a different language of love.

Jacob learned it first—the language of protection.

Thomas learned it through imitation — the language of reflection.

Justin learned it through patience — the language of peace.

Hailey learned it through observation — the language of gentleness.

Lynnlee learned it through joy, the language of wonder.

And Harper, in her baby way, learned it through presence—the language of belonging.

Even Madison, who came to us later, learned the language of inclusion the kind that doesn't have to be taught, only shown.

And Payton, steady and kind, learned it through intention the language of understanding. The kind that listens first, waits quietly, and chooses to stay.

Each one of them built a bridge, not always graceful, not always steady, but real. Sometimes that bridge looked like a video game controller passed quietly across a couch, or a shared bowl of broccoli that made Tyler laugh. Sometimes it was a song, a trampoline, a whispered, "It's okay, he just needs a minute." And sometimes it was just sitting beside him in silence when words didn't reach.

There were years when guilt shadowed me. When I worried that the other kids were growing up in Tyler's wake instead of alongside him, waiting through therapy sessions, adapting to schedules, and learning early how to tiptoe around storms. I wondered if they resented me, or him, or the invisible weight that came with being the "typical" sibling in a house that revolved around one child's needs.

But they surprised me. Again, and again.

Because what I saw as a sacrifice, they turned into strength.

What I feared would make them bitter made them kind.

What I thought might harden them softened them instead.

They grew up understanding that love doesn't always speak out loud. That sometimes it hums. Sometimes it rocks. Sometimes it hides behind routines and rituals that don't make sense to anyone else. They learned to celebrate in whispers, to measure progress in heartbeats instead of milestones.

I like to think of it this way: we each lived on different sides of Tyler's world, me on the outside, trying to reach in, and them growing up inside it, learning its rules instinctively. Between us stretched a bridge made of laughter, patience, and persistence. They became my guides just as much as I was theirs. Together, we crossed and recrossed that bridge every day.

This chapter belongs to them: the brothers and sisters who built their lives around love that looked a little different. The ones who never saw Tyler as less, only as their own.

And it started, like all good stories in our house do, with Jacob. The protector. The first bridge.

Jacob: The Protector

Jacob has always been Tyler's protector. From the very beginning, he took care of his brother: making bottles, fetching diapers, shadowing therapists, and somehow always knowing what Tyler needed before I did. Even as a little boy, he seemed to understand that his brother's world required extra gentleness.

One of my favorite memories of them together still makes me laugh to this day. Jacob must have been six, playing in the backyard with Tyler when they dug up an old doll buried in the dirt. It was one of those strange, half-broken toys kids leave behind, but to Jacob, it looked suspiciously like Jesus.

Before I could even ask what was going on, Tyler picked up the doll and—true to form—brought it straight to his mouth. Jacob's eyes went wide with horror.

"Tyler, no! We do NOT eat Jesus!" he yelled, dead serious.

Tyler froze for half a second, then burst into uncontrollable laughter. For weeks after, he went around telling anyone who would listen, "No, no! We're not going to eat Jesus!"

Even now, at twenty years old, he still says it. Sometimes he'll walk through the house and tell the cat, "Oreo, no eat Jesus!" Or he'll correct his baby sister Harper when she mouths her toys: "No way, Harper, don't eat Jesus!" The story has become family legend, part of our shared language, a silly echo of childhood that never quite fades.

But Jacob's love for Tyler hasn't just been funny moments and laughter. It's been fierce, steady, and sometimes heartbreakingly mature.

During the years after my divorce, when we lived in a tiny house in a tiny town, Jacob became Tyler's anchor. Those were fragile years: years of rebuilding. Tyler struggled deeply with change and hated to leave the comfort and predictability of his dad's house to stay with me. The noise, the lack of space, the uncertainty it all unsettled him.

The only thing that made it bearable was Jacob. Tyler wouldn't come to my house unless Jacob promised he'd be there too. Jacob was entering his preteen years. He was discovering who he was and craving independence. He spent time with friends. Sometimes, he needed what we called a "Tyler break." This was time alone, away from the responsibility of being the big brother to a sibling who depended on him completely.

We'd tell Tyler gently, "It's okay, buddy. Jacob just needs a little break. He'll be back soon."

Somehow, that phrasing stuck. Tyler began calling them "Tyler breaks."

It sounds sad, but to him it made sense, a translation that turned distance into something he could process. He understood it as, "Jacob will come back. Jacob always comes back." And he always did.

When Jacob returned, they picked up right where they left off: pretending to fish in the yard, drawing side by side, or battling zombies on the game console like no time had passed.

Now, years later, not much has changed. Jacob is twenty-two, and Tyler is twenty. Their bond still runs deeper than words. It might be a shared video game, a quiet fishing trip, or a quick stop by the house just to say hi, but Jacob always finds time.

He's still the protector he was at two years old. Still the steady hand, the patient voice, the quiet constant that Tyler trusts the most.

Sometimes I watch them together now, two grown men laughing about old video games, and I realize Jacob never stopped being his brother's bridge. He just learned to carry that role quietly, without needing to be asked.

Jacob's Reflection

Tyler has affected my life in so many ways and I'd like to say they've all been incredible. Whether I need someone completely unbiased to talk to or just a friend who can always make me smile, Tyler has always been that person for me.

He's been my best friend forever, and it makes me so happy to see how far he's come. We still talk about everything we always have, whether it's World of Warcraft, Family Guy, or food, we can go for hours.

I hope he knows I will never need a "Tyler break."

I love Tyler more than anything and would do anything to keep him happy.

Thomas: The Mirror

Thomas and Tyler were close in age, just ten months apart, and for years, they were practically twins. They looked so much alike that people used to argue with me about it in grocery stores. "No, really, they have to be twins," they'd insist. I stopped correcting them after a while. In many ways, it felt true. They learned to read together, were potty trained together, shared toys, shared clothes, shared space, and sometimes even shared the same trouble.

There was a rhythm to their childhood that only they understood. Tyler's world could be overwhelming, but with Thomas beside him, it often felt less so. Thomas moved through life with this light, quick humor and wit, a charm that could disarm anyone. Tyler, who sometimes struggled to connect with others, mirrored that energy. If Thomas laughed, Tyler laughed. If Thomas wore red, Tyler wanted red. They were reflections of each other, sometimes indistinguishable, sometimes wildly different, but always connected.

When Tyler started therapy, the house filled with flashcards and charts, timers and schedules. We did our best to include the younger kids, to make them feel part of the process instead of lost inside it. But some days, the focus fell heavily on Tyler, and no amount of love could erase the imbalance. Thomas was little, but he felt it. He wanted the same attention, the same eyes on him.

So one day, when a strange little behavior started up, a sound, a motion that felt like one of Tyler's stims, we automatically assumed it was Tyler. It went on for days, then weeks. When we finally realized it was Thomas, the truth unraveled slowly. He hadn't lied exactly; he just hadn't corrected us.

There were talks, lessons, quiet apologies. But looking back, I don't see mischief. I see empathy. Thomas wanted to be part of Tyler's world, even if it meant borrowing his rhythm. It was his way of saying, "See me too and see that I see him."

That kind of connection is rare: not imitation for attention, but an early form of understanding. The way twins sometimes swap places without speaking.

At school, their connection evolved into something deeper. Thomas became Tyler's protector, but not in the typical sense. He didn't fight or confront; he deflected. When classmates whispered or stared, Thomas would jump in with humor, clever, quick, and disarming. He had a way of redirecting attention, spinning the story before it could turn unkind.

He used laughter as a shield. And over time, Tyler learned to do the same.

They shared clothes, shared space, shared a rhythm. They spent years in the same school before Tyler transitioned to homeschooling, but even then, the connection stayed strong. Thomas found his passion for theater: lights, scripts, characters, and stories, and Tyler followed along from afar. He learned the names of the plays, the parts Thomas played, and the lines he rehearsed. Even if he never sat in the audience, he could tell you everything about every show.

It's still that way. Their connection doesn't always look loud, but it runs deep, a quiet understanding, a mirrored loyalty. Thomas, with his big presence and humor, and Tyler, with his quiet steadiness, have always been each other's balance.

They are, and always will be, two sides of the same coin, one reflecting light, the other grounding it.

Thomas's reflection

Growing up with Tyler as my big brother has taught me more than I can put into words. He's always been the most confident person I know, unshaken, unapologetic, and never afraid to speak his mind. Being around that kind of certainty showed me how to find my own voice too. Tyler isn't just my brother; he's my reminder that strength doesn't have to be loud to be powerful. He's a role model, an inspiration, and proof that being yourself is the bravest thing you can ever be.

Justin: The Guardian

If Thomas and Tyler were twins in spirit, then Justin was the spark that came right after the daredevil, the rule-pusher, the curious one who couldn't help testing every boundary just to see what would happen next.

He was a few years younger but born with the kind of energy that filled a room before he even spoke. Where Tyler thrived in structure, Justin thrived in chaos. If there was a tree, he'd climb it. If there was a puddle, he'd jump in it. If there was a "no," he'd probably ask "why not?" before his feet hit the ground.

Tyler didn't always find this amusing.

By the time Justin was two or three, noise had become one of Tyler's biggest challenges. Every crash, shout, and laugh from his little brother seemed to set his nerves on edge. Justin's world was loud; Tyler's needed calm. Their personalities collided daily; one was trying to create sound, while the other was desperate to escape it.

Still, even in those early years, they found each other.

Their connection wasn't built on similarity but on balance. Tyler's rules anchored Justin, and Justin's wildness stretched Tyler's world wider.

Tyler was literal to his bones, black and white, right and wrong, rules and routines. And when Justin broke a rule (which was often), Tyler took it personally. "No, Justin! That's not the way!" he'd cry, his voice full of both exasperation and heartbreak. To him, rules weren't just structure; they were safety. Justin, of course, thought he was just having fun.

There were days when their differences felt like too much. Tyler would retreat to his room, muttering about "noise" and "rules," while Justin paced the hallway, confused and hurt, not understanding how love could feel so complicated. But then, as they grew, something shifted.

Somewhere between cartoon marathons and shared book series, their worlds began to overlap. Tyler never aged out of the things that brought him joy, and Justin, to his credit, never asked him to. They bonded over the same shows, traded theories about the same characters, and laughed at the same jokes. What once separated them became what united them.

The boy who once drove Tyler crazy became the person who understood him best.

Now, they share a room and somehow, it works. The same kid who used to test limits is now the one enforcing them. Justin makes sure his friends include Tyler, that they are kind, and that they respect his boundaries and preferences. He notices things others might miss: when Tyler's voice gets too quiet, when the noise is too loud, and when something small has shifted in his routine.

If someone crosses a line, Justin is there. Not with anger, but with loyalty. Quiet, unshakable loyalty.

They have their jokes, their late-night talks, their shared playlists. They talk about girls and games and what they'll cook next. They tease each other like brothers do, but the undercurrent is always the same: protection.

It's almost poetic, really, how the wild one became the steady one. How the boy who once pushed every boundary now guards them fiercely, especially when it comes to his brother.

Somehow, Justin went from the rule-breaking little brother to the roommate, the confidant, and the best friend who makes sure the world stays gentle with Tyler.

Justin's Reflection

Tyler and I have more memories than I can recount.

We've almost shared a room our whole lives, and even when he came to live with us again, instead of saying he should stay in the library, I wanted him in my room. At the time, I didn't know why I said that but later, I realized how strange it felt not having him nearby.

About six years ago, when we lived in Loretta, I remember waking up to Tyler freaking out and having a breakdown. Instead of getting mad at him, I walked over and calmed him down in a gentle way. That's something I don't think many other eleven-year-olds would have done but for me, it was natural.

People often ask what I've learned from Tyler. But to be honest, I've learned just as much from him as I have from any of my other siblings. Growing up with someone who has autism has its benefits. It's taught me how to better help people with disabilities.

But more importantly, it's shown me this:

When you see someone like Tyler or anyone with a disability, your first thought shouldn't be, "Oh, he has autism," or "Oh, he's in special ed."

Your first thought should be:

"That's my friend. That's my partner. That's my companion."

And for me that's my brother.

You might ask, "Justin, what should you do when you meet someone with a disability?"

The answer is simple: nothing at all.

Yes, try to stay calm if they do things that might annoy you but that they can't control. But remember they are human too. Be kind to them. Treat them as equals, just as you would your friends and family.

And above all never make them feel like an outsider.

Hailey: The Caretaker

By the time Hailey came along, our house had already weathered years of therapy schedules, routines, and charts. She was born into the rhythm of it all: the laminated calendars, the sensory tools, and the little trampoline in the hallway. But instead of being overwhelmed by it, Hailey found her place inside it with the kind of grace only a child could have.

She adored Tyler from the very beginning. Where other kids might have seen a brother who was different, she saw someone who just needed a little extra care, and she was more than happy to give it. In many ways, Hailey became a little mother to him.

When she was small, she shared everything with Tyler: her toys, her snacks, her stories. She'd hand him dolls or figurines, building elaborate worlds of imagination while he sat beside her, content to line them up or hold one quietly in his hand. They didn't always play the same way, but somehow, they still played together. It wasn't about matching each other's worlds; it was about being willing to sit in both.

Hailey was full of imagination, a born storyteller who could turn a stack of blocks into a kingdom and a cat toy into a royal scepter. Tyler wasn't one for pretending, but he would sit beside her, humming softly, occasionally chiming in with a fact about cats or a line from a show they both loved. That was his kind of pretend: facts and rhythm, order, and joy.

When Hailey outgrew the cartoons he still loved (Blue's Clues, VeggieTales, and Dora the Explorer), she didn't leave them behind completely. Once a week, she'd curl up on the couch beside him and watch anyway. Not because she still wanted to but because he did. It was her way of saying, "I see you."

They've always shared a love of cats. Between the two of them, our home has become a revolving door of rescues, fosters, and strays. Every time a new cat wandered into the yard, Hailey's big eyes would find mine, and Tyler would stand beside her as backup. "We should keep it," she'd say sweetly. "It's cold." Tyler would nod solemnly, adding, "Yes. It's hungry." And that was it; I didn't stand a chance.

Even now, they have their inside jokes, their shared laughter that bubbles up when no one else gets the reference. Hailey loves all things spooky: skeletons, Halloween movies, ghost stories, but Tyler has made it his mission to "educate" her on better options. He'll lecture her about alternative movies, explain why certain storylines "don't make sense," and roll his eyes at her horror playlists. She humors him, laughing, pretending to take notes. It's their ritual, a playful debate wrapped in sibling love.

Hailey has always been the sunshine in his shadow, and he's her quiet protector in return. When her friends come over, Tyler watches from the edge of the conversation, curious and polite. But when a boyfriend shows up, his protective instincts kick in full force. He watches every move like a silent security guard, making sure things don't get "weird."

If Hailey laughs too loudly or belches, Tyler immediately corrects her with mock seriousness, "Hailey, that's gross," in the same tone I imagine I used on him years ago. And when she rolls her eyes, he grins because they both know what it really means.

It means he loves her.

He might not always say it, but he shows it in the way he notices her, the way he hovers nearby, the way he makes sure she's safe, respected, and never forgotten.

Together, they remind me that love doesn't have to look the same to be felt the same.

Sometimes, it's a shared cartoon. Sometimes, it's a rescued cat. Sometimes, it's a brother standing quietly nearby just to make sure everything is okay.

Lynnlee: The Reflection

Lynnlee is a world all her own: a beautiful, complex, extraordinary little pond that no one else could ever quite replicate.

She and Tyler share a bond that defies explanation. Maybe it's because, in their own ways, they see and experience the world through the same kind of lens, the one that magnifies sound, color, and feeling until it's almost too much. Maybe it's because they both crave calm, quiet, and certainty in a family that's anything but predictable. Or maybe it's something simpler: they just get each other.

Lynnlee is also on the spectrum. Now, it's called "Level 1" high functioning. She is "Twice Gifted" or E2. She's social but sensitive. She's capable but can get overstimulated easily. Tyler was diagnosed with what they used to call "classic" or "infantile" autism, now considered "Level 3," the kind that impacts every layer of life. The world likes to label them differently, to measure the distance between their levels and categories. But inside our home, they exist on the same wavelength.

Both are brilliant. Both feel deeply. Both are quick to withdraw when the noise of the world becomes too much.

If I let them, they'd both retreat into their own little corners, content in the quiet. Tyler with his shows, his rhythm, his structure; Lynnlee with her coloring books, headphones, and gentle humming. They would coexist in peaceful silence, not lonely, just still.

But I don't let them stay there forever. I pull them out, gently, patiently finding small ways to bring them back to each other and to us. And what I've learned is that when they do meet in the middle, it's magic.

Tyler shows a patience with Lynnlee that he rarely shows with anyone else. He teaches her how to cope when the world feels too loud, how to hum, how to breathe, and how to use rhythm to regulate. I think he sees in her the same fight he's already fought, and maybe, in helping her, he finds a kind of peace.

And Lynnlee, for her part, brings out something in Tyler that's hard to describe. Maybe it's gentleness. Maybe it's pride. Maybe it's the quiet relief of being understood without having to explain.

They talk about food a lot: ramen noodles, pizza, snacks they both love, like a shared language only they speak. They debate which SpongeBob episode is the funniest, rewatch old Full House reruns, and argue lovingly about which character they like best. To anyone else, it might sound like a quirky age-gap friendship. But to me, it's something sacred.

There's something both heartbreaking and breathtaking about watching your twenty-year-old and your six-year-old bond over the same simple joys. They laugh at the same punchlines. They love the same characters. They both find peace in the predictability of reruns and the comfort of routine.

Sometimes I catch them sitting side by side on the couch, Tyler with his calm, steady hum and Lynnlee mimicking him quietly without even realizing it. It's like watching two frequencies align, harmonizing in a way that no one else in the world could ever replicate.

As their mom, it fills me with something I can only describe as a grateful ache.

It breaks my heart that they face the same struggles: sensory overload, a need for order, and a pull toward isolation. But it also heals me to know they share something else: understanding. They are proof that love doesn't just adapt; it evolves.

Tyler, once the little boy everyone worked so hard to reach, now reaches out himself. And Lynnlee, the little girl born into a family already shaped by his journey, teaches him what connection looks like when it's met with instinct instead of effort.

They are two halves of the same melody, one that began decades apart but somehow landed in perfect rhythm.

Lynnlee: The Reflection (continued)

If you ask Lynnlee what she thinks about Tyler, she doesn't hesitate.

She doesn't list diagnoses or talk about sensory issues or routines. She just looks at me like I'm the one who doesn't understand and says, matter-of-factly:

"What do you mean? Tyler is normal, Mom. You are so weird. And Harper is very loud."

It makes me laugh every time. But it also stops me in my tracks. Because in that one sentence, she said what the rest of the world still struggles to see.

To her, Tyler isn't "on the spectrum." He isn't "different." He's just Tyler, her big brother who watches cartoons with her, shares snacks, helps her calm down, and makes sure she's okay.

The world will always try to categorize them: to separate, measure, and define. But Lynnlee has already decided what really matters. To her, her brother is just normal.

And maybe that's the most hopeful reflection of all: a generation that doesn't see lines to cross, just people to love.

Madison: The Chosen Sister

When Madison came into our lives, I was scared.

Not because of her, but because she was so close in age to Jacob and Tyler, and I worried she might not want to deal with all that came with him.

When she met Tyler, he was in one of his hardest seasons: the depths of puberty, hygiene struggles, constant stimming, emotional ups and downs, and the fights over deodorant and routines. All the things that make adolescence complicated for any family turned up to ten.

But Madison didn't flinch.

Where most people might have pulled back, she leaned in. She embraced him with patience and a quiet kind of love that asked for nothing in return. She laughed with him, listened to him, and gave him space to just be Tyler.

They even had their own special ritual: "hand hugs."

Tyler didn't want to go to bed without one. He'd press his palm against hers, fingers to fingers, and whisper, "Hand hug."

It wasn't just a routine. It was safety. It was his way of saying, "You make me feel seen."

Madison became that safe place for him. Someone who chose him, not someone assigned to him by birth. That mattered more than I think she'll ever know.

He'd give her movie recommendations: Disney films, old animated classics, anything he loved, and she'd watch every one, coming back later with "reviews" just to let him know she'd really listened. It was their shared language, built on popcorn and inside jokes.

And fast food runs? Those were their thing. Car rides, fries, laughter—the kind of simple memories that root themselves in your heart without you even realizing it.

To Tyler, Madison wasn't a "stepsister." She was his person, the one who met him where he was and never asked him to be different.

And maybe that's the truest definition of love: not the kind you're born into, but the kind you choose, over and over again.

Madison's Reflection

Tyler has taught me that autism doesn't stop anyone from doing anything.

He's a super movie genius he can tell you anything about movies, TV shows, or actors without even having to look it up.

Having Tyler in my life has changed me in so many ways. He's helped me have more patience and taught me to never underestimate anyone.

Tyler is the sweetest, most loving person I know and has a heart of gold.

My life wouldn't be complete without Tyler or our hand hugs.

Payton: The Patient Brother

Payton entered Tyler's world quietly; no big gestures, no forced connection, a steady presence. He came into our family the same time as Madison, and from the start, he understood that loving Tyler wasn't about fixing him or figuring him out. It was about showing up.

Where others might have tried to draw Tyler out, Payton learned to walk beside him instead. He noticed the small things, like when Tyler's voice rose in excitement over a movie scene or when he needed a little extra space after a long day. Payton didn't push. He waited. He listened.

There is something rare about the kind of patience Payton carries. It is not loud or demanding. It is quiet, consistent, the kind that builds trust one ordinary moment at a time.

Sometimes that looked like watching the same YouTube reviews Tyler loved, just so he could talk to him about it later. Sometimes it meant sitting in comfortable silence while Tyler talked to himself about baseball stats or superhero timelines. Payton never mocked it, never rolled his eyes. He understood that this was conversation. Tyler's version of reaching out.

And slowly, something soft grew between them. Respect. Familiarity. Brotherhood.

He's never had to declare his love for Tyler. He lives it in the small, steady ways that say, "You're worth knowing."

Maybe that's his gift: to teach that real connection doesn't have to be loud or instant. Sometimes, the quietest kind of love is the one that lasts the longest.

Harper: The Littlest Shadow

Harper doesn't see Tyler as different. She just sees him as hers.

At three years old, she doesn't have labels or definitions, only love. To her, Tyler is the big brother who still loves Blue's Clues, who will sit on the floor and play with her toys for hours, and who always comes running when she calls his name.

And he really does come running. Every time.

If she calls from the playroom, he appears within seconds not out of obligation, but out of instinct. He checks on her, helps her reach things, and lets her climb onto his couch when the world feels too loud.

He'll hand her his iPad when she asks, and somehow, she always knows exactly which buttons to press, even when the rest of us can't figure it out. They have a quiet understanding, the kind that doesn't need words.

Sometimes I watch them together and wonder if Tyler sees something in Harper that no one else can. Maybe it's her innocence, or maybe it's that she doesn't expect him to be anyone but himself. She never tries to fix him, teach him, or question him. She just loves him loudly, clumsily, and honestly.

Tyler is selfless when it comes to Harper. He shares, he plays, he teaches, and he comforts her with the same tenderness I once used to comfort him. He protects her fiercely, almost like she's his child instead of his little sister.

Unless, of course, ESPN is on.

Or a Texas team is playing.

Then, Harper becomes "the annoying little sister" who talks during the game. And she doesn't mind; she'll just sit beside him anyway, mimicking his expressions and pretending to cheer when he does.

Sometimes, when I catch them together, her tiny frame beside his, both of them giggling at some private joke, I realize something that still stops me cold:

Harper will grow up never knowing a world where she has to "accept" her brother. She was born into one where love already existed.

And maybe that's the most beautiful legacy Tyler could ever give her.

Closing Reflection: The Family That Love Built

When I look at my children now, grown, growing, scattered across their own worlds, I see how every one of them has been shaped by Tyler, and how, in their own way, each has helped shape him too.

Jacob taught him loyalty — the kind that doesn't fade when life gets hard.

Thomas taught him humor — how laughter can disarm a room faster than words ever could.

Justin taught him protection — how love sometimes looks like standing guard.

Payton taught him patience — the quiet kind that waits, listens, and stays, even when words fall short.

Hailey taught him imagination — how to sit beside someone and make pretend feel real.

Lynnlee taught him reflection — how to see yourself in another soul and offer grace.

Madison taught him choice — that love isn't bound by blood, but by how you show up.

And Harper… Harper taught him what it means to give love freely, without questions or conditions.

Together, they built something that no therapy, no intervention, no program ever could.

A family that understands love doesn't have to be loud to be real.

Ours is a house where laughter and chaos coexist, where the trampoline once shook the floors, and where the smallest gestures, like a hand hug, a shared joke, a quiet moment between cartoons mean more than milestones ever could.

For years, I thought my job was to hold Tyler's world together.

But looking back, I see that they all did it for each other.

The brothers, the sisters, the chaos, the calm; each one is an anchor in their own way.

They learned early that love doesn't require perfection, only presence.

And through it all, Tyler wasn't the center of our storm.

He was the calm that taught us how to weather it.

So, when people ask me what it's like raising a child like Tyler, raising siblings around autism I tell them this:

It's like building a home out of mismatched bricks, each one chipped, each one beautiful, each one essential.

It's love layered in every direction: backward, forward, sideways; the kind that doesn't just hold but heals.

And somehow, in all that noise, motion, and grace.

We became a family not in spite of autism.

but because of it.

The Shadow Binder

The Weight of Paper

The first binder was heavy. But this one was worse.

The zipper rasped when I opened it, that low, plastic snarl that always raised the hairs on my neck. The scent was familiar too: a cocktail of toner, coffee, and recycled air from years of waiting rooms. When I set it down, the case thudded against the tile, the sound sharp enough to startle the cat. Sometimes, when I dragged it behind me in my tote on wheels, the clack-clack over the grout lines kept rhythm with my heartbeat. It didn't just carry papers; it carried everything I couldn't say out loud.

There were nights I'd unzip it just to check that nothing had been left behind. Each divider glared back at me like a chapter I didn't choose to write. This was what motherhood had become: signatures instead of lullabies, assessments instead of bedtime stories. I used to hum over a crib; now I memorized federal codes. Love had turned into paperwork, bound in three rings of steel.

The Shadow Binder wasn't a binder anymore; it was a fortress. A portable archive of every battle I'd fought for Tyler, every door slammed in my face, and every letter I'd written at 2 a.m. It was thicker, darker, and meaner than the first. The first binder had been my shield; this one was my weapon.

It lived in a black zippered case because a regular three-ring binder couldn't contain it anymore. I used to carry it in a tote bag, but eventually it got its own rolling case, like a business traveler who'd overstayed his welcome. It sat in place of the first binder on a high shelf. If the first binder was proof of survival, The Shadow Binder was proof of war.

Order and Chaos

Years had passed since that first IEP meeting where I'd slammed papers down and dared a principal to argue with her own documentation. I was older now, sharper. I didn't cry before meetings anymore. I didn't second-guess myself. I knew the rules, the deadlines, and the loopholes. I could quote federal special education law better than some advocates.

But every page I added to The Shadow Binder was a reminder that for every year Tyler grew taller, the bureaucracy grew taller too. I started color-coding tabs: green for occupational therapy, yellow for ABA notes, red for speech evaluations, blue for district-level communications. Tyler's life was reduced to a rainbow of data points. And yet, despite all that organization, the binder still felt chaotic, bulging at the seams like it could barely contain him.

The dining room became command central. The table that once hosted birthday cakes and art projects was now buried under legal pads, Post-its, and half-drunk coffee cups. There were nights when dinner was served on paper plates balanced between stacks of forms, the glow of my laptop replacing candlelight. Every color of highlighter meant something: green for progress, pink for deadlines, and yellow for warnings.

The binder didn't rest. It traveled from room to room with me, from kitchen to car, from meeting to meeting. It sat open beside my plate at dinner, crumbs of toast wedged between the pages. There were mornings when I'd wake with a pen still in my hand, ink smudged across my wrist. The sound of the printer became the soundtrack of our lives, sheets spitting out judgments and jargon while cartoons played in the next room. I kept thinking that if I could just organize it enough, label it, categorize it, color-code it, maybe the world around us would start to make sense too.

But order was an illusion. The more precise I became, the more chaos found its way in. Motherhood had split into two versions: the one who made therapy schedules and packed lunch boxes, and the one who battled bureaucrats with a three-inch binder as her sword. I was on a mission to unite with other families fighting the battle and to change things once and for all.

Data vs. Real Life

One of the heaviest sections was the "Behavioral Data" tab. Pages and pages of charts with dots and numbers, tracking meltdowns and triggers like he was a science experiment. Each dot was a day I'd lived through, holding him as he screamed, shielding him from lights, noise, the weight of the world, and yet on paper, it looked clinical. Cold.

The graphs were supposed to measure behavior. They never measured recovery. One chart showed a spike on a Tuesday, the day the vacuum cleaner broke and the noise sent Tyler into orbit. What the chart didn't show was what came after: me sitting cross-legged on the hallway floor with him in my lap, whispering that he was safe until his breathing slowed. It didn't show the way he'd trace my wedding ring after every meltdown, grounding himself in its smooth circle.

The data made our life look clean, manageable, contained. But living it was messy; it was sticky fingers, tear-stained shirts, Lego landmines under bare feet. Those tiny dots and percentages couldn't capture the laughter that often followed the storms, or the way he'd apologize by pressing his forehead against mine, wordless but full of meaning. On paper, he was a pattern of triggers. In real life, he was a boy trying to make peace with a world that never stopped buzzing.

The Shadow Binder wasn't just paper. It was a shadow of me.

I carried it everywhere: in waiting rooms, in the backseat of the car, into every meeting. My back ached from hauling it, my fingers calloused from flipping tabs and reprinting records. Every time I zipped it up, I felt like I was locking away another piece of myself.

Reflection in the Glass

One day, I caught my reflection in a window while lugging it into a district office. My hair was messy, my shoulders slumped under the weight. I looked like I was dragging luggage through an airport after a red-eye flight. Except I wasn't going on vacation; I was walking into another room full of people who saw my son as a problem. In the window's reflection, I saw it clearly: I'd become the binder. Overstuffed, scuffed, patched together with tape and stubbornness. The same exhausted durability. The binder bore dents from doors; I bore wrinkles from worry. Both of us had survived years of being hauled through spaces that didn't want us. There was a strange comfort in that recognition. It reminded me that maybe we were both still standing because we refused not to.

I hated that binder. But I needed it more than air.

The Shadow Binder had its own legend in our house. The kids knew not to touch it. Tyler would run his fingers along the zipper sometimes, fascinated by its size, but he never opened it. To him, it was just "Mom's folder." He didn't know that inside were reports calling him "maladaptive," "rigid," "defiant." He didn't know there were pages that broke me, pages that made me sob in the parking lot before I could drive home.

One report in particular haunts me. It was a behavioral assessment from a school psychologist who had only met him twice. The first line read:

"Tyler's prognosis for meaningful progress is limited."

I remember staring at that sentence until the words blurred. Limited. That's how they saw him. That's what they wrote in permanent ink. Another person who thought my child would max out, who thought he had limits. A person who chose not to learn how to communicate with him and be in his world, so they wrote him off as limited.

I didn't show that page to anyone. I tucked it behind a stack of legal documents in the back of the binder, but I could still feel it there, like a bruise under the skin.

The Trial

There was a day I brought The Shadow Binder to a meeting that felt more like a trial than a parent-teacher conference.

That morning, I sat in my car in the school parking lot, binder seat-belted beside me like a second passenger. I'd dressed in my "meeting clothes" (you know the ones): the good jeans, the cardigan that made me look calm instead of combative. My stomach was a knot. The radio played softly, some forgettable song that I couldn't turn off because silence made my thoughts too loud.

I watched the building's double doors swing open as staff filed in, coffee cups in hand, laughter echoing. To them, it was just another Tuesday. For me, it was battle day. I touched the binder's handle, took one deep breath, and whispered, "Let's go."

Inside, the fluorescent lights hummed, and the hallway smelled like dry-erase markers and lemon cleaner. The wheels of the binder rattled against the tile as I pulled it behind me. Every step felt like marching toward judgment.

By the time I sat down at the long table, I was steady. The shaking stopped. They had no idea I had already rehearsed every argument in my head the night before, whispering lines in the bathroom mirror between brushing my teeth and tucking the kids into bed.

It was a district-level review, the kind where they gather administrators, specialists, and lawyers because you've pushed too hard and they want to push back. There were twelve of them and one of me. The table was lined with laptops, legal pads, and polite smiles that didn't reach anyone's eyes.

I placed The Shadow Binder on the table like a gavel.

The district rep cleared her throat. "We're here to review Tyler's case," she began. "We've evaluated his recent progress and believe it may be appropriate to transition him into a more independent classroom environment."

Translation: They wanted to cut support. Again. Even though two weeks prior I had a call that he was pulling his pants down in his one little thirty-minute "mainstream" class. He did this because there was no resource support, there was no advocate, and there was one teacher to the 32 students. One of those 32 told Tyler he was supposed to pull his pants down when he knew the answer. Tyler simply did not know it was inappropriate and listened.

So I unzipped the binder slowly, like a scene out of a courtroom drama, and pulled out a document from the previous month. "That's fascinating," I said, sliding it across the table. "Because this says he still requires one-on-one assistance for safety in group settings. And this," I flipped to another tab, "says he's regressed in fine motor skills since moving just 30 minutes of instructional time last semester."

The district rep glanced at the papers but didn't meet my eyes.

"Would you like me to pull the therapist's report too?" I asked sweetly, already reaching for the next tab.

By the time I was done, the table was covered in documents. The Shadow Binder sat open like a dragon guarding treasure, daring anyone to challenge me.

Tyler kept his support that year. But I walked out of that building shaking, my chest tight with rage and adrenaline. I wasn't just a mom anymore; I was a one-woman legal department with a rolling briefcase.

The Breaking Point

But the scariest battle came when the school failed me and him in the worst way.

They'd "forgotten" to notify me of an IEP meeting. No email. No call. Nothing. And because I wasn't there, they voted to "mainstream" him. No notice. No consent. Just a rug yanked out from under our feet.

I found out when Tyler came home from school exhausted, withdrawn, and confused. I started asking questions, and within hours I was back at that school demanding answers. The truth was ugly: Tyler had been dumped into a general education classroom without proper support, without transition planning, and without me there to fight for him.

And that's when the bullying started.

A boy in that class thought it was hilarious to convince Tyler that it was okay to threaten people. That it was funny to say he wanted to kill people. Something he had never heard before. So, when he threatened to shoot someone and that boy told his parents, I got a call.

The teacher tried to cover it up. But when you have four older brothers in the same school, nothing stays secret. Within days, I knew everything.

Two days later, Tyler was back in his safe classroom. They threatened expulsion; I threatened lawyers and discrimination. I went federal, and all of a sudden, his previous IEP was active again; they honored all of his resources, and he was back to his routine with the teachers and friends who made him feel safe.

But the damage was done. Parents had heard about the pants-pulling and the "violent" threats. One family even threatened to press charges. Tyler was mortified but couldn't explain himself. He didn't understand why everyone was upset. He didn't know why they were angry with him.

And that's when The Shadow Binder saved us.

I brought it to the district office and slammed it open on the table. I had documented meeting minutes proving they had failed to notify me. I had evaluations from multiple specialists describing his vulnerability to suggestion. I had pages showing that he was not developmentally able to discern right from wrong in situations like this.

I had notes from parents with similar children and parents in the mainstream class. All advocating for Tyler like my tiny army of heroes.

That binder didn't just tell Tyler's story. It exposed theirs.

By the end of the meeting, the school was apologizing. The teacher was reprimanded. The boy was disciplined. And Tyler's record was cleared.

The meeting ended with apologies, but they felt thin. Paper-thin. I gathered my binder, slid the papers back into their tabs, and walked to the car in a daze. The late afternoon sun hit my face like a spotlight, too bright after hours in fluorescent air. When I sat down behind the wheel, I didn't start the engine. The binder sat in the passenger seat, its corners pressing into the fabric like it was claiming territory.

I wanted to feel triumphant. I'd won. But instead, I felt like a soldier counting casualties. My throat burned from holding in everything I wanted to scream. Somewhere inside that binder was the proof I'd needed, but it came at the cost of peace.

I drove home on autopilot, radio off, my mind replaying the moment they'd said "expulsion" like it was a threat instead of a wound. When I pulled into the driveway, I just sat there, hand on the gearshift, whispering, "You're safe now," though I wasn't sure if I meant him or me.

There's a part no one warns you about: the space between victory and collapse. When the meeting is over and the signatures dry, when the doors close behind you and the adrenaline drains out, you're left with silence. Not peace. Just silence. The kind that hums in your ears and makes you realize how long you've been running on fumes.

For years, I told myself it was worth it. And it was. Every service, every accommodation, every inch of progress wrestled from a system built to resist. But there were nights I'd sit on the edge of my bed and wonder what else it had cost. My marriage cracked under the pressure of constant defense. My body carried stress like a second heartbeat. Even my other kids learned to read my mood by the way I handled the binder; if I slammed it down too hard, they'd go quiet. If I set it aside gently, they knew it had been a good day.

Tyler didn't see the toll. He just saw me showing up. And maybe that's what mattered most. But I sometimes wish he'd known how many times I sat in parking lots, forehead pressed to the steering wheel, crying over decisions made by people who barely knew his name.

There's a fatigue that comes from fighting the same battle a thousand different ways. It seeps into your bones, into the way you breathe. But there's also a strange grace in it. You start to realize that advocacy isn't about winning every fight; it's about making sure your child never feels like they're fighting alone. If you're lucky, maybe they never realize it was a fight at all.

I used to imagine what it would feel like to live a life without binders. To wake up and not have to plan my day around paperwork, calls, and meetings that decide whether my son gets the help he deserves. But then I remember: those binders are a testament. To him. To me. To the years when love had to be louder than policy.

I'm not ashamed of the fight anymore. I just wish the world hadn't required it.

The Shadow Binder wasn't just paper anymore. It was power.

The Cracks Between Pages

There were moments that never made it into the binder, the ones too raw to file, too human to summarize. The reports showed progress and regression, but they never captured the in-between, the quiet collapses that built up over the years until we finally closed it for good.

By eighth grade, the cracks in the system were wide enough for my son to fall through. There were the "supervised" bathroom breaks where the aide waited outside instead of going in, and the day another student punched Tyler in the stomach while no one was watching. Each time, we got apologies, forms, and promises. But the pages never changed. The binder grew heavier, and Tyler grew quieter.

So, we stopped.

We closed the binder, shut the case, and decided to bring him home. Homeschool wasn't part of the plan; it was the only way forward. Not because I thought I could teach better, but because I couldn't stomach sending him back into a world that called itself inclusive while leaving kids like him unprotected.

This isn't a story about blame. Most of the teachers and aides were doing their best. But "best" still left bruises, still let moments slip by that shouldn't have. The truth is, awareness doesn't fix everything. There are still gaps wide enough for kids like mine to disappear into, and parents still have to climb down after them.

The Shadow Binder taught me how to fight. But closing it taught me something harder: how to let go of a system that was never built for him and build something new from scratch.

The Weight and the Light

The binder grew heavier each year. Pages multiplied. Reports stacked up. What started as a tool to get services became a timeline of everything the system had failed to give him without a fight.

But it wasn't all pain. Some pages were small victories, handwritten notes from teachers who loved him, progress charts showing leaps we'd prayed for, and glowing comments from therapists who saw the Tyler I knew. Those pages mattered too. I laminated a few of them, as if to protect them from the weight of the rest.

Still, the binder had a shadow over it. Because the thicker it grew, the harder it was to see my son as more than a case number. It was as if the binder followed me, whispering: This is who he is on paper. Don't forget.

And I hated that. Because I knew the truth: no binder, no matter how big, could capture the boy who narrated backyard races like an ESPN commentator, who belly-laughed at broccoli jokes, who whispered "Mama" in the dark when words were still rare.

One night, after a particularly brutal meeting, I sat in the living room with The Shadow Binder on my lap. The house was quiet. Tyler was asleep upstairs, his breathing soft and even, finally at peace. I flipped through the pages like someone flipping through a photo album, except there were no smiles here. No milestones written in joy. Just evaluations, scores, and deficits.

I ran my hand over the cover and whispered, "You don't get to define him."

Then I zipped it shut.

The Shadow Binder taught me more than the system ever meant to. It taught me that advocacy is exhausting, ugly, and relentless, but it's also sacred. It taught me that I could walk into a room of a dozen professionals and not blink. It taught me that love sometimes looks like paperwork, like late-night emails, like knowing federal law by heart.

It also taught me that I would never be the mom who let the world decide who her child was.

The binder is still here, tucked away next to the first one in a plastic storage bin in the attic. When I see them side by side, I feel a mix of pride and grief. They're like gravestones, markers of the years we survived.

But there's a difference now. The first binder scared me. The second one made me strong.

It is a shadow, yes, but it's also a shield. And even though I hope I never have to open it again, I know I will if I need to.

Because I've learned something The Shadow Binder will never understand:

Sometimes, on quiet days, I still climb up to the attic. The air smells like dust and old cardboard. Light filters through the vent in narrow stripes that fall across the two binders, one white, one black, stacked beside boxes of baby clothes and faded report cards. I'll brush the dust from their covers, my fingertips tracing the indents of years-old labels.

They aren't trophies. They aren't gravestones either. They're proof of every time love had to turn itself into evidence. They remind me of who I was when I didn't think I could keep going and did anyway.

Tyler's laughter drifts up from downstairs, deep and unguarded. I smile, keep the case closed, and whisper, "You don't own us anymore."

The zipper slides shut with a sound that feels final. The attic settles into silence, but this time it feels like peace instead of weight.

My son is bigger than every word inside of it.

Reflection

I'm not ashamed of the fight anymore. I just wish the world hadn't required it.

Even now, after all the progress and awareness, the fight hasn't disappeared; it's just changed shape. The forms are digital instead of paper, the meetings sound gentler, but the exhaustion feels the same.

Somewhere, a mom is still learning the law at midnight. Somewhere, a dad is still walking into a meeting, praying someone listens. Awareness may have given us language, but it hasn't yet given us peace.

For every parent still in the battle, those just starting their binder, and those too tired to lift it anymore, I see you. The world is better, but not yet good enough.

And that's why the binder stays in the attic. Not because I expect to use it again, but because I know someone else still has to.

Puberty and the Awkward Years

Flash-Forward Remarriage & New Trust (2018)

By twelve, life looked different.

I had remarried. My husband stepped in steadily and patiently, the way Tyler needed people to be. Change usually unraveled him. With him, it didn't. Trust grew one repetition at a time.

One night Tyler braced in the hallway, refusing the shower. I started my usual dance, but my husband crouched beside him. "Looks hard tonight," he said softly. No push. No shame. He stood, turned on the light, and sat on the tub's edge. "I'll go first. Make sure it's safe." He got in, clothes and all. He washed his own arms. Lathered his own hair. "Shampoo is just soap that sings," he said matter-of-factly, counting a slow sequence: one arm, two, belly, back. Reset when Tyler flailed. Start again. Love in our house looked like a sequence, not speeches.

One day it clicked. Tyler showered on his own. Again, the next night. Again. Before the month ended, he showered twice a day and put on deodorant without a prompt. We didn't throw a party. We traded a look across the kitchen, "Did you hear?" and ate microwaved leftovers like a feast. I'd spent years teaching people how to meet Tyler where he lived: therapists, teachers, even family. Every connection was earned through handouts and explanation, a translation of how to see him. And then here was someone who didn't need the manual. No speeches. No warnings. He just showed up, steady as breath. He listened more than he spoke, mirroring Tyler's pace without realizing he was doing it.

One night I caught them in the hallway, side by side at the sink. Tyler's reflection hovered in the mirror, cautious, copying my husband's movements: toothpaste first, rinse second, towel third. No prompts, no pleading. Just rhythm. Watching them, something inside me unclenched. Maybe love didn't have to be earned or translated. Maybe it could just exist, fluent in its own silence.

Later, folding towels, it hit me that Tyler wasn't the only one learning to trust again. I was too. And that's what healing really looks like: not a finish line or a breakthrough, but two people learning, slowly, to stop flinching when kindness shows up.

People saw a "typical" twelve-year-old. They didn't see the years of sweat and patience behind that click.

The Battle of Hygiene and Self-Awareness

If puberty had a soundtrack, ours would have been the squeak of deodorant caps, the slam of bathroom doors, and me yelling, "Use SOAP this time!" from down the hall.

The hygiene wars nearly broke me.

Tyler was fifteen, technically, but in some ways, he was still the kid who hated the sound of running water, the scratch of towels, and the sting of toothpaste that was "too spicy."

Now throw in body odor and hormones. It was like living with a confused caveman who quoted SpongeBob and ESPN.

He hated showers. Not because he was lazy, but because they were sensory nightmares.

The water was "too loud." The steam made his skin "itchy." The shampoo felt like "slime."

Every step was a battle.

I tried everything: different shampoos, noise-canceling headphones, and warm towels ready afterward.

Some nights, we'd negotiate like diplomats.

"Quick shower, five minutes, no conditioner," I'd bargain.

He'd sigh, stomp to the bathroom, and yell over the door, "I'm clean!" thirty seconds later.

He wasn't.

I once sniffed his hair and said, "Tyler, you smell like outside and chicken nuggets."

He thought about it and shrugged. "That's not bad."

And honestly? He had a point.

But hygiene wasn't just about smell; it was about self-awareness.

Puberty brought changes he couldn't ignore, but he didn't understand them either.

He didn't know when deodorant was needed or why lotion helped dry skin.

He'd wear the same shirt for three days in a row because it "felt safe."

Once, before school, I handed him a clean shirt. He sniffed it, frowned, and handed it back. "This smells like Target."

He went back to his "safe shirt," worn, soft, and absolutely ripe.

There were days I cried in the laundry room because I didn't know how to teach something so basic without shaming him.

How do you say "You smell bad" without saying "You are bad"?

So, we built systems.

Charts. Checklists. Visual schedules.

Each one is laminated, color-coded, and taped to the bathroom wall:

Brush teeth

Wash hair

Use soap with water.

Deodorant (both sides!)

He loved checking off boxes. Progress was measurable. And little by little, it worked.

He started remembering on his own. He started caring, even if just a little.

Then one day, he came out of the bathroom smelling like clean linen and asked, "Do I smell good?"

I hugged him. "You smell amazing."

He grinned. "I did well."

And just like that, I forgot every battle we had fought.

Puberty, for us, was never just awkward. It was a sensory warfare clash between independence and overload.

But underneath all the struggle, there was progress. Real, slow, stubborn progress.

The Smell of Change

Puberty was not gentle in our house. It didn't knock politely on the door; it crashed through it, armed with body odor, awkward stares, and the kind of questions that make you pray for a parenting manual written by someone braver than you.

Tyler hit puberty like he hit everything else in life at full speed and completely unfiltered. One minute, he was happily watching Blue's Clues with a juice box; the next, he was asking me why the lady on Baywatch was running so fast in slow motion.

He didn't understand what was happening to his body, or his mind. He just knew things felt… different. He didn't know why his skin crawled when he was embarrassed, or why sometimes he couldn't stop staring at girls in tank tops at Walmart. He didn't know there were rules, invisible ones, about what you can say out loud or where your eyes are supposed to go.

And I didn't know how to teach them.

You know how awkward it is to talk to a typical fifteen-year-old boy about erections, attraction, hygiene, and personal space?

Now imagine having that conversation with someone who still wanted to carry a Handy Dandy Notebook in his backpack. Someone whose world still revolved around SpongeBob and ESPN2, but whose hormones had decided to enroll in an R-rated biology class without permission.

He'd ask questions at the worst times, loudly, publicly, and without shame. Once, in the checkout line, he looked at a woman's chest, then turned to me and said, "Mom, she's got two big muscles." I wanted to disappear into the gum rack. But he wasn't being rude; he was observing. The same way he'd notice the shape of clouds or the color of a car.

He'd also panic about his body's new smells, hair appearing where it hadn't before, changes he couldn't control. For a child whose world thrived on predictability, puberty was a betrayal. His own body had broken the schedule.

That's when I learned that puberty wasn't just biology for Tyler. It was sensory overload. New textures, new sensations, new emotions. He'd sniff deodorants like he was in a lab, reject twenty before accepting one that didn't "smell spicy." He'd scream if his armpits felt sticky, refuse showers because the water temperature was never "exactly right."

It was chaos. Beautiful, awful, hormonal chaos.

And through it all, there were moments that broke my heart and made me laugh at the same time, like catching him sitting cross-legged on the bed, Blue's Clues playing softly on the TV, while he asked in total seriousness, "Mom, how do you know if you're in love or just hungry?"

The Talk No One Prepared Me For

There are a lot of things motherhood doesn't prepare you for, but this? This was a master class in uncharted territory.

There is no chapter in What to Expect When You're Expecting called "How to Explain Erections to a Boy Who Still Sleeps with His Blue's Clues Blanket."

No therapist, no IEP, no parenting manual, no late-night Google search could have prepared me for it.

Tyler approached "the talk" the way he approached everything: curious, literal, and completely unfiltered. He didn't want metaphors or euphemisms. He wanted diagrams, definitions, and timelines.

He'd catch me off guard with questions that belonged in a health textbook but came out of nowhere.

Once, as I was stirring spaghetti sauce, he asked, "Mom, what exactly does mating season mean?"

Another time, he interrupted a family movie night to ask, "How do you know if you're supposed to marry someone or just say hi?"

He wasn't being silly. He was trying to decode a world that ran on rules no one had ever explained to him: social rules, emotional rules, physical rules. His brain, so logical and literal, needed instruction manuals for feelings.

I tried my best. I bought a few books written for teens with autism about puberty and relationships, bright covers, simple sentences, cheerful drawings of stick figures wearing deodorant. We read them together, page by page. The trouble is no two people are alike, and autism doesn't change that. My story will be completely different from anyone else's.

He'd nod, frown, then ask the kind of follow-up questions that made me want to fake a phone call.

"So… if a girl hugs you and you get erect, does that mean you love her or that she's warm?"

He was so serious.

And I wanted to laugh (I did laugh, once or twice), but mostly, I wanted to cry. Because behind his confusion was a quiet, growing awareness: he knew he was different. He knew there were things other kids just got that he had to study like homework.

We practiced conversations the way we used to practice flashcards.

"What do you say if someone tells you they like you?" I asked.

He'd think hard, then reply, "Cool."

"Okay, but maybe say thank you, too."

"Oh. Thank you. Cool."

We built scripts for situations that would have come naturally to others: what to do if a girl flirted, what to do if a teacher talked about dating, and what not to say about bodies in public.

He didn't always get it right. Once, at a restaurant, he told a waitress she had "a symmetrical face," and when she smiled awkwardly, he beamed, "That means you're beautiful, scientifically."

He wasn't wrong. He just didn't know the rules.

I learned that puberty, for Tyler, wasn't just physical. It was social puberty, emotional puberty, sensory puberty: layers of change that collided all at once. Maybe this is how it is for us all; Tyler just didn't know to keep it in his head. He was asking the questions most young boys probably have.

And every question, every uncomfortable conversation, every awkward encounter became a chance to build a bridge between his world and mine.

Sometimes he'd circle back days later with one of those unexpected, out-of-nowhere reflections that reminded me just how much he was absorbing.

Like the night he came into my room, leaned on the doorframe, and said, "Mom, I think love is when you care if someone eats lunch." Then he shrugged and walked out like he hadn't just said something profound.

And I realized: maybe puberty wasn't about teaching him to understand everything. Maybe it was about teaching me to understand him as he changed: messy, beautiful, literal, and entirely his own.

Friends, Not Dates

For most parents, puberty brings the terror of first crushes, heartbreak, and teenage romance.

For me, it brought the terror of trying to explain that just because someone smiled at you doesn't mean you are supposed to propose.

Tyler didn't date not because he couldn't, but because friendship made more sense to him. Romance was too abstract. Friendship was structured, predictable, and safe.

He liked people who made him laugh, who talked about sports or TV or food. The rest? It confused him. He didn't understand the gray areas: the "maybes," the "I think she likes you," or "it's complicated." Tyler didn't do "complicated." He did yes or no, black or white, like or dislike.

There was one girl in particular; I'll call her Hannah. She was kind and patient, one of the few classmates who never laughed when he repeated things or stimmed in class. She sat with him at lunch sometimes, shared her chips, and listened to him talk about ESPN and fantasy football.

To Tyler, this was love.

One afternoon, he came home glowing. "Mom," he said, "I think Hannah and I are getting married."

I smiled carefully. "Oh yeah? What makes you think that?"

"She said she liked my shirt."

That was it. That was the data point. Compliment equals commitment. Case closed.

I didn't laugh, at least not then. I wanted to protect that innocent logic, that pure way he saw connections.

Because the truth is, Hannah did care about him. But she was also a teenage girl, juggling social codes that Tyler didn't understand.

And when her friends teased her, asking why she sat with "the weird kid," she started sitting somewhere else.

Tyler noticed immediately.

He came home, sat down on the couch, and said, "Mom, I think Hannah got traded to another team."

He said it with the same matter-of-fact tone he used for football updates.

And it broke me.

Puberty had brought him something I wasn't ready for: rejection.

It wasn't dramatic, it wasn't loud, but it was heavy. The kind of heartbreak that doesn't come from romance, but from realizing the world doesn't always return your kindness.

We talked about it that night. I told him that sometimes friends move on, and it doesn't mean he did anything wrong. He nodded, not crying, just quiet.

Then he said, "That's okay. Maybe she'll come back when she's ready for lunch again."

I tried to talk more, but he told me I had too many words and went to watch football.

That was Tyler, hopeful, forgiving, and still somehow steady.

As he grew older, his relationships remained simple and honest.

He didn't play games. He didn't pretend. He loved people the way he loved everything, fully and without a filter.

When friends drifted away, he didn't hold grudges. He just said, "They're busy," and went back to his routine.

But his siblings noticed. Jacob, Thomas, and Justin would step in, pulling him into group hangouts and making sure he was included. They understood how those small exclusions could sting, even if Tyler didn't show it.

Sometimes, late at night, I'd catch him scrolling through photos on his iPad: family pictures, friends, and old teachers. He'd whisper little updates to himself, like he was keeping track of everyone.

It wasn't loneliness, exactly. It was connection, in his own quiet way.

He once told me, "Friends are like favorite songs. You don't have to listen to them every day. But when you do, you still know all the words."

And I realized maybe he understood friendship better than any of us.

Because puberty didn't turn him into someone new. It just revealed what was already there: his loyalty, his empathy, his endless capacity for unconditional love.

The Mirror Moments

There comes a time in every parent's life when you realize your child has started seeing himself not just in mirrors, but in the eyes of others.

For most kids, that moment is subtle: a glance in a store window, a sudden self-consciousness about a haircut, and a hesitation before smiling for a photo.

For Tyler, it came like a thunderclap.

He was sixteen when it really hit him.

He'd always been aware of routines, of rules, of fairness, but not of difference. For years, "autism" was just a word adults used in meetings. It wasn't him. It wasn't personal.

Then one night, he stood in front of the bathroom mirror, toothbrush in hand, staring at his reflection longer than usual.

He said, softly, "How do people know I'm different before I say anything?" Then, in his typical way, he would answer himself, "Because you are Autism Tyler."

It stopped me cold.

He wasn't angry, just curious, maybe a little sad.

He'd started noticing how kids at the grocery store would whisper. How teenagers his age would laugh when he spoke too loudly or flapped his hands in excitement. How girls smiled politely but never stayed long.

And there I was, standing in the doorway, trying to find words big enough to hold his question.

"They don't really know you," I said carefully. "They just see what they don't understand."

He nodded, thinking. "Tyler knows Tyler."

"Yes," I said. "And that's what matters."

But even as I said it, I could see something changing in him.

For the first time, he saw himself not just as Tyler, my Tyler, the boy who could quote every SportsCenter episode. He was also someone finding his place in a world that didn't always recognize his value.

Those mirror moments came more often after that.

Once, at a family gathering, his cousins were laughing and joking about girlfriends. Tyler sat quietly for a while, then blurted out, "I don't think I'll get married. I think I'll just have ESPN."

Everyone chuckled, but I saw the truth hiding underneath it.

He was protecting himself from rejection by turning it into a joke.

Another time, he watched Jacob leave for a new adventure in adult life; he asked himself, "Will I ever move out?" Then he answered himself with brutal honesty, "No Tyler, mom makes your food; you can't use the oven; the oven gets too hot."

It wasn't about independence; it was about belonging. About wanting the same milestones everyone else took for granted.

I told him he'd move out when he was ready. That his path might look different, but it was still his.

He smiled and said, "Okay. Maybe I'll just live next door."

And honestly, that sounds perfect to me.

Still, those moments hurt.

There's no manual for when your child first recognizes the world's unfairness.

It's the kind of heartbreak you can't fix with therapy, charts, or advocacy binders.

All you can do is stand beside them and make sure the mirror they look into reflects love, not lack.

I made a quiet promise to myself that night:

If the world ever made him feel small, I'd make sure home always made him feel infinite.

So, we filled the house with laughter again.

We leaned into the things that made him shine: his encyclopedic sports knowledge, his kindness, and his ability to make anyone smile.

I made sure he knew that "different" wasn't a wound; it was a wonder.

Because the truth is, the world doesn't get to define what normal looks like.

Tyler does.

What Stayed the Same

Puberty changed a lot about his voice, his body, and his routines.

But it didn't change him.

Even in those awkward years, when deodorant felt like a personal attack and social rules were a foreign language, the core of who Tyler was never wavered.

He still lined up his DVDs by color. He still hummed the SportsCenter theme while brushing his teeth. He still asked if the broccoli was steamed "just right."

Sometimes, I'd find him on his bed, sitting cross-legged. He held a Handy Dandy Notebook in one hand and an iPad in the other. He was half little boy, half young man, narrating his own imaginary Blues Clues: Sports Edition.

His voice would deepen mid-sentence, cracking between childhood and adulthood, but his joy stayed the same.

And that, more than anything, reminded me that growth doesn't always mean outgrowing.

For Tyler, it meant expanding and making room for new experiences without losing the comfort of old ones.

He still wanted hugs, though now they came with a mumbled "I'm too old for this" under his breath.

He still needed structure, but he also started making his own.

One night, I found him scribbling a handwritten "daily plan" in a spiral notebook.

Wake up

Brush teeth

Breakfast

ESPN

Check on Harper before she stops being a level zero.

Text: Mom, "hi"

Dinner

Sleep

It was his version of control, a quiet way to anchor himself in a world that kept asking him to adapt.

Sometimes, I'd get glimpses of the man he was becoming flashes of maturity that caught me off guard.

He'd comfort Hailey after a bad day, cracking jokes until she smiled.

He'd remind Lynnlee to take deep breaths when she was overstimulated.

He'd even scold Justin for leaving dishes in the sink, like a grumpy dad.

But then, the next moment, he giggled at SpongeBob or held a plushie to his chest, whispering something that only he understood.

And I realized: there's no finish line between childhood and adulthood. There's just life, unfolding in its own rhythm.

People love to say things like, "He's come so far."

And while that's true, it always feels incomplete. Because Tyler hasn't just come far; he's stayed true.

Even when hormones turned his emotions into whirlwinds and his body betrayed his comfort zone, he stayed gentle. Stayed kind. Stayed Tyler.

There was a night, right around his seventeenth birthday, when he sat beside me on the couch, taller than me now, and said, out of nowhere, "I think I'm okay."

I asked what he meant.

He shrugged. "Just… me. I'm okay being me."

That one sentence carried more weight than any progress report, any therapy milestone, or any binder full of goals ever could.

Because that's what every fight, every sleepless night, every meeting, every tear was for: not perfection, not progress, just peace.

The truth is, puberty didn't break him. It didn't even bend him.

It just peeled back another layer of who he was always meant to be: self-aware, self-possessed, and quietly extraordinary.

And it didn't break me either.

Those awkward years taught me to let go, to stop chasing normal, and to stop trying to fit my son into a box built for someone else's comfort.

It taught me that "growing up" doesn't always look like moving on. Sometimes it looks like holding on to laughter, to love, and to the parts of ourselves that make us feel whole.

So much has changed since then: his size, his schedule, his playlists; but every once in a while, when the house is quiet, I'll hear him in his room.

The faint bounce of his old trampoline.

The low hum of the ESPN theme.

The soft, steady rhythm of a boy who never stopped being exactly who he was.

And I smile.

Because through every change, every awkward stage, and every messy in-between

What stayed the same was everything that mattered.

Before Autism Was a Hashtag

The Diagnosis Era

Tyler was officially diagnosed in early 2009.

The day we got the diagnosis didn't feel like a revelation. It felt like a courtroom sentence.

The clinic smelled faintly of antiseptic and burnt coffee, the kind of smell that clings to old magazines and nervous hands. The fluorescent lights buzzed overhead, their hum mixing with the rustle of paper as the doctor flipped through Tyler's file.

He didn't look at me when he said it. He just adjusted his glasses, cleared his throat, and read from the chart like a man delivering bad news from a safe distance.

"Severe Infantile Autism."

He said it flat, clinical, and final.

Not "your son has autism." Not "your son is autistic." Just a label dropped on the table like a gavel's strike.

The word "infantile" hit harder than severe. Infantile meant never growing up. Never changing. Never moving forward. I remember staring at the letters on the page as if they could rearrange themselves into something softer.

He kept talking about "long-term prognosis" and "lifelong care," but all I could hear was the hum of the lights and the sound of my heart pounding in my ears. I looked at Tyler, sitting on the cold exam table, spinning the tongue depressor like it was a toy airplane. He wasn't listening. He didn't care about charts or labels. He was humming under his breath, lost in his own little rhythm.

I wanted to ask what severe meant. Did it mean he'd never talk? Never read? Never live on his own. But I didn't. I was twenty-five, and this man had a degree and a clipboard. I just nodded and tried to swallow the fear crawling up my throat.

There was no warm hand on my shoulder, no packet of resources, no "you're not alone." He handed me a stack of printouts, told me to "call the early childhood program," and walked out.

That was it.

No roadmap. No hope. Just a word that would change everything.

On the drive home, the papers slid off the passenger seat, scattering across the floorboard. I remember pulling over, gathering them up, and staring at one line printed in bold:

"Child presents with severe deficits in communication and social reciprocity."

Deficits. That was the first word they gave me to describe my son.

Back then, autism wasn't something people wore on T-shirts or hashtags. It wasn't spoken about on podcasts or packaged into classroom "sensory corners." Autism wasn't mainstream; it was misunderstood, misnamed, and often ignored. And that made our fight even lonelier.

Before Awareness Was Marketable

Back then, autism wasn't something people wore proudly or printed on puzzle piece coffee mugs.

There weren't social media posts with colorful captions about "neurodiversity" or "awareness months." There was no language for what we were living. Just stares, assumptions, and silence.

Before autism was a hashtag, it was a mother trying to quiet her screaming child under the cold lights of Walmart while strangers whispered. It was a toddler lying flat on the tile floor, pounding his fists, and a young mom too scared to explain because she didn't even have the words yet.

If you walked into a grocery store in 2009 and saw a meltdown, you didn't see sensory overload; you saw a "bad kid." That was the story people told themselves because it made them comfortable.

One Sunday after church, an older woman told me, "You just need to teach him who's the boss."

She said it with a smile, like she was offering wisdom.

I smiled back, holding Tyler's hand as he flapped and rocked beside me. I didn't have the strength to explain that discipline couldn't fix sensory pain, and I would have done anything to make his world feel safe.

Once, in a restaurant, a man leaned over his booth and muttered, "You people don't believe in spanking anymore, huh?" I wanted to tell him that the only thing hitting Tyler would accomplish was breaking me.

Now, people film meltdowns for awareness, add captions about sensory overload, and share them with hashtags and compassion. But back then, we hid in bathroom stalls until it was over. Progress looks different when you've lived through both.

There was no manual, no "top ten strategies for autism parents" list. There was just instinct, exhaustion, and love so fierce it bordered on desperation.

Every outing was a risk. Every sound a trigger. Every stranger a potential wound.

When the world saw a meltdown, I saw survival. When the world saw disobedience, I saw pain.

And the hardest part was that no one else did.

Before autism was a hashtag, it was my son screaming in the middle of Walmart.

Before Jenny McCarthy. Before TikTok advocacy. Before sensory rooms in schools and Instagram reels of awareness campaigns, there was just me, Tyler, and a storm of confusion no one wanted to name.

The Military Silence

We were living on base pay, barely scraping by. I was twenty-one, with Jacob on my hip, Tyler in the cart, and Thomas still kicking around in my belly. My back ached. My ankles were swollen. And Tyler, not yet one, was arching his back in the cart seat and screaming. Not because he wanted candy. Not because he wanted a toy. But because of the lights. The noise. The overstimulation that had no name in my vocabulary. Sensory overload is a newer term than many care to admit.

The stares always came before I even saw them. That look people give you when they think your kid is "bad," or when they think you are. One woman passed me in the cereal aisle, looked me up and down like I was gum stuck to her shoe, and said loud enough for everyone to hear, "You should just whoop him more." Then, with a glance at my stomach, she added, "Should've thought of that before having kids without a dad."

She didn't see the uniform hanging in our hallway back home. She didn't know we couldn't afford wedding rings. She didn't ask why my son couldn't handle the lights and noise of a Walmart. To her, I was just another young mom with no discipline, no husband, and no control.

Even doctors didn't take me seriously. In the early 2000s, autism wasn't handed out like candy. It wasn't handed out at all. It was avoided. Ignored. Shoved under the rug. Especially in the military. Autism wasn't something they treated; it was something they transferred. If your kid was too loud, too disruptive, too inconvenient for the image of discipline, they didn't offer support. They just moved you somewhere smaller, quieter, farther away, where no one had to see. This also meant no support, no help.

The military taught me discipline, but it never taught me how to fight this kind of war.

You learn early on that silence is safety, that order is everything, and that image means more than truth. Autism didn't fit their image. It didn't march in straight lines or salute at the right times. So instead of addressing it, they buried it.

When I started asking questions about services, therapy access, and respite care, I was met with blank stares and thin smiles. "Ma'am, we'll look into it," they'd say, which was military speak for no one's going to help you, but we'll make you think we might.

I remember one meeting with a base pediatrician who told me, "He'll grow out of it. Boys mature slower." He said it like a reassurance, as if maturity could untangle neurology. I nodded politely, holding Tyler in my lap while he covered his ears from the buzz of the fluorescent lights.

Another time, I asked about occupational therapy; he blinked like I'd spoken another language. "Ma'am, we don't have that here," he said, flipping through Tyler's chart. "Maybe try a speech pathologist when he's older."

Older. Always later.

But autism doesn't wait for later. It takes root in the early years, in the moments when intervention can rewrite a lifetime.

We were stationed in a nowhere town, three hours from the nearest developmental clinic. There were no specialists, no sensory gyms, no early childhood centers. I spent hours on hold, calling every number I could find, and being transferred from one department to another like a ghost in the phone lines.

When I finally found a center two states away that offered evaluations, they told me the waitlist was fourteen months. I remember hanging up and sitting on the kitchen floor, Tyler spinning beside me, wondering how many milestones he would miss while we waited for a phone call that might never come.

That was when I stopped waiting.

I learned to make flashcards. I read research studies until 3 a.m. I begged for referrals. I called senators' offices, commanding officers, anyone who would listen. I was tired of being the polite military wife. So I became the loud one.

People whispered that I was "difficult." That I "made things harder for myself." Maybe I did. But if being difficult meant my son got help, then so be it.

Because the truth was simple: Tyler didn't need to be cured; the system did.

The Fight for Change

There is a kind of strength you don't find in gyms or boot camps; the kind that is born in waiting rooms.

The kind that builds one phone call, one rejection letter, and one breakdown at a time.

That's where I found mine.

The breaking point came after yet another denial. A letter stamped in bold red: "Does Not Qualify."

It was addressed to the parent or guardian of Tyler, as if even the envelope couldn't be bothered to know my name.

They said he was too young for therapy, too "uncooperative" for testing, too something for everything.

I remember standing in the kitchen, letter shaking in my hand, staring at the refrigerator where Tyler's therapy goals were taped up beside crayon drawings of stick figures and pumpkins. One of his goals read: "Respond to name when prompted."

He'd done it once that week. I'd cried like I'd won the lottery.

And now they were telling me it wasn't enough.

I tried everything I could name—diet changes, baby signing, therapy waitlists that stretched months long. And when nothing worked, I cracked. I called a priest. I asked him to bless our house because I didn't know what else to do. He sprinkled holy water across the threshold while I whispered, "Please, just help him sleep."

Because he didn't sleep. And neither did I.

Back then, autism was painted as one thing: low IQ, low function, lost causes. Tyler didn't fit that picture. He didn't speak, didn't point, didn't follow instructions. But he could solve puzzles meant for middle schoolers. He saw patterns in chaos. He remembered things I didn't even know he'd seen. The system had no place for that contradiction. And when the system didn't know what to do with you, it ignored you.

Until you make noise.

So I started making noise.

I fought for respite care not just for the EFMP child but for their siblings, something no military mom with a neurotypical kid ever had to think about. I fought to change regulations so they couldn't station special-needs families in cities with no resources. I wrote letters. Filed paperwork. Showed up. Not because I wanted to be a hero. But because I was tired of feeling like a secret they wanted to bury.

Tyler fought every day to survive in the world. So I fought to change it.

It began with a single email. Then ten. Then fifty. I sent them to anyone whose title started with "Command," "Office of," or "Department of."

When they didn't respond, I called. When they didn't answer, I called again.

I wasn't trying to start a movement. I was trying to save my child. But sometimes, the two are the same thing.

By the time someone finally listened, I was on a first-name basis with an aide from the Department. She told me my case wasn't unique, that there were hundreds of families like ours stationed in towns without services, waiting over a year for an evaluation.

That number lit something in me.

I drafted letters. I started collecting stories. I spoke in acronyms because I'd memorized them all: EFMP, EDIS, IDEA. I could recite them like scripture.

At night, after the kids were asleep, I sat at the dining table surrounded by papers and coffee cups, typing statements until my wrists ached.

And then, one afternoon, the phone rang. A voice on the other end said, "Ms. we've reviewed your documentation. You were right. We're revising the policy." It wasn't just me fighting this across the country. Some determined moms were also pushing for change. Together, we secured resources.

I didn't even realize I was crying until my face hit my hands.

They changed it.

We were heard.

The new regulations required early intervention access before relocation, no more transferring families into therapy deserts. It wasn't just a win for us. It was for every parent who'd ever been told to "wait."

But even victory comes with grief.

Because by the time those changes went into effect, Tyler had already lost years. Years we'd never get back.

He was four by then. Still mostly nonverbal. (Nonspeaking now.) Still struggling with sounds that other kids had mastered before kindergarten.

Every word was a mountain. Every glance, a miracle.

The system that should have helped him had taught me something instead: that love can be louder than bureaucracy. That one mother with a binder and a backbone can move the needle, even when the machine tries to swallow her whole.

And I swore, right then, that I would never stop being loud.

When Awareness Finally Came

But I wasn't just raising a child with autism. I was raising him before the world even had a name for what he was going through. There was no hashtag, no podcast, no Facebook group swapping therapy wins and meltdown tips. If you wanted advice, you went to a library. If you wanted empathy, you waited a long damn time.

I didn't have a village. I had a diagnosis no one wanted to give and a baby no one wanted to understand. People didn't say "neurodivergent." They said "difficult." "Delayed." "Wrong." And the label didn't come with resources. It came with isolation.

And yet somehow, Tyler still smiled. He still looked at me like I was his safe place. Even when the world was too bright, too loud, too unforgiving, he found me. And I found him.

So no, there wasn't a ribbon. There wasn't a month or a social media campaign. There was just a boy spinning in the grocery aisle and a mother holding the line while the world looked away.

I didn't know how to fix it. But I knew how to fight.

And sometimes, that was the only awareness that mattered.

When the world finally learned the word "autism," it felt like a victory I didn't know how to celebrate.

Suddenly, there were ribbons, T-shirts, and fundraisers.

There were awareness months and color-coded puzzles on every corporate logo.

There were hashtags that went viral, influencers who filmed meltdowns for empathy points, and therapists who finally had waiting lists long enough to prove how far behind the world had been.

Part of me was grateful.

Finally, people cared.

Finally, there were conversations, funding, and early intervention centers on every corner.

But another part of me, the part that remembered sitting in that empty clinic waiting room, holding a screaming toddler while no one knew his name, felt something different.

A quiet bitterness.

A grief that came years too late.

Because while the world was discovering the beauty of neurodiversity, I had already lived the ache of its invisibility.

I had fought for inclusion before anyone knew the word.

I had been called "crazy," "dramatic," "too much," long before advocacy became a profession.

And I had the scars and the binders to prove it.

When awareness finally came, I realized it was never the word I wanted, anyway.

Awareness is passive. It's a glance. A nod. A "that must be hard."

What I wanted was acceptance.

Understanding.

A world that didn't need a label to show compassion.

Now, when I see posts about sensory kits in classrooms or watch teachers proudly share their "autism inclusion" trainings, I smile. Because those things matter. They're progress.

But I also remember when teachers rolled their eyes. When I had to beg for aides. When I carried a three-inch binder into meetings because no one believed me.

Awareness came, but it came riding on the backs of mothers like me.

Mothers who carried their children and their paperwork through decades of disbelief.

Mothers who made noise in systems built to silence them.

Mothers who didn't wait for hashtags.

And I'm proud of that.

Because when I look at Tyler now, his humor, his intelligence, the way he navigates a world that still struggles to understand him, I see proof that awareness was never the goal.

He was.

He always was.

The world may have finally caught up, but he has been leading the way all along.

Final Reflection — The Quiet Before the Hashtag

Before autism had a ribbon, it had a heartbeat.

Before it was a word on a screen, it was my son's laughter echoing through the grocery aisles.

Before it became awareness, it was survival.

Before it was celebrated, it was misunderstood.

I used to think the world needed to see him to understand him.

Now I know it's the other way around.

Because awareness didn't make Tyler whole, he always was.

What it did was catch a small glimpse of the brilliance that had been there all along.

Every milestone, every fight, every binder, every sleepless night, it was never for applause or hashtags.

It was for him.

For the boy who taught me that advocacy isn't about making noise.

It's about making sure no one else has to scream just to be heard.

And maybe that's the real awareness.

Not the colors. Not the campaigns.

Just love, loud enough to change the world.

We have awareness now we are battling for acceptance and understanding.

The Echo of Everything

I like to watch him with the younger kids and the pets.

There's a rhythm to it now, one I've come to recognize like a song that only our house knows the words to. The calm way he moves, the way he presses his palms against his thighs when he's thinking, the little hum that sneaks out between his sentences. The air in the room changes when he's in it. The chaos slows down just enough to find its own kind of order.

He talks to Oreo, our cat, like they've been best friends for years. Sometimes he even gives Oreo a voice, feminine and serious.

"Oreo says we should get more treats," he'll tell me, without looking up from his tablet. "But only the crunchy ones; soft treats make her lazy."

Oreo meows, probably because her name has just been mentioned, and Tyler nods solemnly, like he's been validated.

Some parents might find it odd.

I find it holy.

Because there was a time I was told I would never hear his voice.

Doctors wrote "nonverbal" in ink that felt permanent. They wrote "severe communication delay," "low likelihood of expressive language development."

They handed me reports that described his silence as if it were a life sentence.

But they didn't know him.

They didn't know that the silence wasn't absence; it was waiting.

Now, it's all I hear.

He narrates his thoughts like a play-by-play commentator.

"Harper's making her move toward the fridge: bold strategy!"

"Lynnlee's drawing another cat in remarkable form, strong lines!"

"Mom's burning toast again, tragic!"

He narrates everything: the grocery runs, the dog walks, even folding laundry. Life, for him, is a running broadcast, a sport where everyone has a role and every moment has a highlight reel.

Maybe for him, life is a sport.

And maybe that's why he calls the play so well.

Sometimes he hums between sentences. It's the same soft hum he made when he was little, the one I used to listen for like a pulse. Back then, it was the sound that told me he was calm, that we'd made it through another storm. That hum is home to me now.

It's steady and low, like the hum of the refrigerator that's been running for twenty years, or the sound of the dishwasher cycling in the background of our conversations. It's the sound of peace disguised as noise.

The mornings are my favorite.

The kitchen smells like coffee and toast. The light that filters in through the blinds is golden and soft, catching in his hair as he sits at the table with Harper. Oreo winds between their chairs, tail curling like a question mark.

Harper's trying to convince Tyler that her cartoon character can fly using "super friendship power," and Tyler is breaking down why that's scientifically impossible.

"Harper," he says seriously, pouring his , "you can't defy gravity with love. That's not how molecules work."

Lynnlee will chime in laughing, wide and bright. "Yes, you can if it's Disney love!"

He tilts his head, considering. Then … "I just wish you would all be level zero."

The way they look at him, like he's the smartest person in the world, still makes me want to cry.

If you freeze that moment, it looks ordinary. A boy, his sisters, cereal bowls, and coffee cups, sunlight. But for us, it's everything.

There was a time when I wasn't sure I'd ever hear him say my name. I used to whisper it when I rocked him at night, testing the sound of it out loud: "Mommy, Mama, Mom," trying to imagine how it would feel to hear it from him.

Now he says it twenty times a day. Sometimes with love.

Sometimes, with exasperation.

Sometimes it's just because he likes to say it.

"Mom, I fixed the remote."

"Mom, the cat is ignoring me."

"Mom, what's for lunch?"

"Mom. MOM. MOOOOM."

Each one is a small miracle.

There's peace in our house now, maybe not quiet peace, but a kind that breathes, that hums. It's a hard-earned peace, built from years of chaos, therapy, schedules, and sheer stubborn love. It's the kind that only comes when you've lived inside the storm long enough to stop fearing the thunder.

He moves through the house like he belongs in every room.

He checks the thermostat every morning because he likes it at exactly seventy-three degrees; seventy-two is too cold, and seventy-four is "gross."

He lines the remotes up on the coffee table, from smallest to largest, perfectly parallel.

He talks to the vacuum cleaner as if it is an employee.

"You're doing great work today," he'll say, patting the top of it when it finishes a room.

When he helps Lynnlee with her math homework, he sits beside her with quiet patience. "Okay, but see, the answer's in the question," he'll tell her. "Mom said I can be a teacher; that can be my job. I will get paid."

Sometimes, she doesn't get it, but she smiles anyway because she loves how he explains things.

Every word, every hum, every sound from him feels like proof that love did what it was supposed to do; it built a bridge.

Sometimes I catch him standing in the doorway, watching the girls play. He doesn't always join in, but he's there, fully present, watching. His hands flap lightly when he's happy. His mouth curves up in that small, soft smile that means more than any sentence ever could.

And when he laughs, really laughs, that deep, contagious laugh that starts in his chest and shakes his shoulders, I swear I can feel it in the walls. It's the kind of laugh that makes the pets perk up and the kids pause mid-argument just to grin at him.

It's still wild to me that there was a time when the only sound I heard from him was screaming hours and hours of screaming that no one could explain. Now, that same mouth tells jokes, gives me weather updates, argues about pizza toppings, and sings along to songs from years ago.

His favorite is still "Where Is My Hairbrush."

He belts it with conviction, windows down, one arm out like a conductor leading a choir of invisible veggies.

I used to dream about miracles…big ones. Now I know they don't arrive in lightning bolts.

They arrive in whispers. In routines. In the steady hum of a boy who once lived in silence.

Sometimes, at night, when the house is finally still and I can hear the faint echo of his voice from his room, I stop outside the door and just listen.

He's talking to himself, narrating his evening, maybe planning tomorrow's tasks. Sometimes he's just whispering the stats of a game he's watched a hundred times.

"Texas won that one," he says softly, "twenty-four to seventeen."

It's not about the score.

It's about the rhythm.

It's about the fact that he's here, speaking, existing, narrating a life that was once lived in the shadows.

That sound: the murmur, the hum, the echo of his thoughts, s the sound of everything we fought for.

It's the sound of everything I ever prayed for.

And as strange as it may sound, I never want the house to be completely quiet again.

Because silence, for us, isn't peace.

It's a memory.

And this, the voice, the laughter, the hum, the echo, is everything that came after.

The World Caught Up (Sort Of)

Autism may be more widely accepted now, and that warms my heart more than I can ever explain.

Sometimes I'll see a billboard or an ad for "Autism Awareness Month," or a school with a "Sensory Inclusion Day," and I'll catch myself smiling at nothing.

Because it means the mothers who fought beside me, the ones who cried in parking lots, who filled binders, who refused to be quiet, were heard.

We were told we were too much.

Too loud.

Too emotional.

Too combative.

But we weren't wrong.

We were early.

Now, the world has started to understand what we always knew: that kids like Tyler don't need to be "fixed." They just need to be seen.

Chuck E. Cheese does Sensory Tuesdays now with dim lights, lowered volume, and no strobe lights. That simple change could have changed our entire childhood. I still remember standing in that pizza place years ago, trying to convince a manager to turn down the volume while Tyler screamed into my shirt. I'd have given anything for a dimmer switch that day.

Now, those switches exist. And every time I see a flyer for "Sensory-Friendly Family Night," I want to hug the mom who made that call, who filled that form, who didn't give up until someone listened. Because I know her. I was her.

There are sensory rooms in schools now, beanbags, soft lighting, fidget bins: things that used to exist only in therapy clinics. Teachers have words for the things I had to describe from scratch.

Back then, I said, "He can't handle fluorescent lights." Now, they say, "He's sensitive to visual overstimulation."

Back then, I said, "He doesn't like crowds." Now, they say, "He needs decompression time."

I watch this shift happening, and I feel both gratitude and grief.

Gratitude because it is working people are learning, listening, and adapting.

Grief, because I wish it had been like this earlier.

If the world had been softer when Tyler was little, maybe I wouldn't have had to be so hard.

But this is what progress looks like. It's uneven, imperfect, but it's movement.

Our home still looks like the one I fought to protect all those years ago. Noise-canceling headphones hang by the door if not on Tyler or Lynnlee's head not because they need them every day, but because they like knowing they're there. A promise of peace, always within reach.

The lights are still dim. The televisions stay low enough that you need the captions. The routines never left us; they just evolved. Lunch still looks the same: same plate, same drink, same rhythm because comfort still lives in the familiar.

People think structure is limiting. But for us, it's freedom.

I keep the walls painted in warm colors: soft grays, faded blues, nothing too sharp or bright. I keep the house smelling faintly of laundry soap and coffee. I've learned the art of background quiet: a dishwasher hum, a soft fan, the steady rhythm of safety.

When guests visit, I warn them: "We don't do loud here. We don't do surprise visits."

They laugh, but they listen. They adapt too.

This house, this life, are a living museum of everything we learned about peace.

Weighted blankets are folded on the couches.

Visual schedules are taped to the fridge.

Cats know when to sit on laps and when to stay away.

This isn't about control anymore. It's about compassion.

I sometimes think of the world outside our door, the one that's finally catching up. The one that's starting to understand the language we've been speaking for twenty years.

Autism isn't whispered now. It's celebrated. People wear puzzle pieces and infinity symbols; they share quotes about neurodiversity and acceptance. There are job programs, college support systems, and adults on the spectrum telling their stories proudly.

It's beautiful.

But it's also strange.

Because for so long, we were told to hide.

When Tyler was diagnosed in 2008, the word autism carried shame, confusion, and even fear. People lowered their voices when they said it. They offered pity instead of understanding. They spoke about our children like they were tragedies.

Now, it's hashtags, T-shirts, and campaigns.

#DifferentNotLess.

#AutismAcceptance.

#NeurodivergentAndProud.

And I love that shift. I do. But sometimes, I can't help thinking about the moms who came before hashtags. The ones who sat in the waiting rooms when no one knew what sensory meant. The ones who were blamed for everything they didn't cause.

We were the rough draft, so this version could exist.

There's power in that, even if it came at a cost.

When I look at Tyler now, this 20-year-old man who reads, jokes, and narrates life like a sportscaster, I see every step of that evolution written in him. He is living proof that awareness became acceptance, and acceptance became inclusion.

He still has his quirks: the rituals, the schedules, the loyalty to ESPN, the specific way he lines his shoes by the door, but the world doesn't stare as much anymore. That feels like a victory.

We didn't end up in an institution like they just knew we would.

We didn't lose him to silence or fear.

We didn't become the cautionary tale whispered in doctors' offices.

We became proof that love, advocacy, and stubborn hope could rewrite a story.

The world caught up. Maybe not perfectly. Maybe not evenly. But it caught up.

There are still moments that sting, moments that remind me that inclusion is a work in progress.

Like when we go to a restaurant and the music is too loud, or when someone rolls their eyes because he's talking too much about the Texas Rangers.

But now, instead of explaining, I just smile. Because I know who he is, and I know we've already won the battles that matter.

Sometimes I'll be at the grocery store and see another mom, younger than me, with a child who's covering his ears under the hum of fluorescent lights. She looks around, embarrassed, defensive. I recognize the panic in her eyes; instantly, it's the same panic I used to feel when the world didn't make space for us.

I always stop. I always smile. Sometimes I whisper, "You're doing great."

And she looks at me like she's been seen for the first time all day.

That's when I know the fight was worth it.

All of it.

Because even if the world doesn't always get it right, it's trying.

And in the meantime, we keep building our own version of peace.

Noise-canceling headphones. Dim lights. Captions on the TV. Cats on the couch.

Our home will always be that safe place.

Our little world is steady, predictable, and kind; the one that helped him thrive long before the rest of the world understood why it mattered.

When I think back on everything the binders, the diagnoses, the battles. I realize the real victory isn't that the world learned to make room for kids like Tyler.

It's that we learned to stop apologizing for needing the room.

We don't shrink anymore. We don't whisper explanations.

We exist exactly as we are a family built from chaos and miracles, structure and love.

He still eats the same lunch. He still hums when he's content. He still loves sports, cats, and broccoli. And I still love him for every bit of it.

Our lives don't look like the world's idea of "normal," and that's okay.

Because normal never raised a boy like Tyler.

And if the world has finally caught up enough to see that, then maybe, just maybe, we're already home.

The Future According to Tyler

When people ask about the future, I used to freeze.

For years, that question carried more fear than hope.

What will happen when he is grown?

Where will he live?

Who will take care of him when you can't?

I used to lie awake at night with that question sitting heavily on my chest.

Not because I didn't believe in him; I always did, but because I knew how unkind the world could be to those who live differently.

Now, when people ask about the future, I smile.

Because Tyler has his own version of it.

And it's perfect.

He wants a girlfriend.

He's not shy about it either. He says it the way some people talk about their dream house: certain, casual, like it's already written.

"I want to get a girlfriend," he tells me, "and work with her. Then we'll get married."

I ask where they'll live, and he pauses, thinking, then shrugs.

"Probably here," he says, like it's obvious.

It makes me laugh every time.

In his mind, life doesn't happen somewhere else. Home is enough.

He wants to work at Whataburger or Burger King, both if he can manage it. He loves the smell of fries, the rhythm of orders, the simple clarity of a job done right.

He doesn't dream of travel, riches, or fame.

He dreams of name tags and aprons, coworkers who laugh with him, and coming home to feed the cats.

He wants a lot of cats. A lot.

He talks about it like other people talk about their retirement plans.

"There will be one named Oreo Two," he says seriously. "And another named Burger. And maybe one called ESPN."

He's already mapped out the feeding schedule.

"Cats don't like change," he reminds me, "so it's important to be consistent."

I don't know where he got that line, but I know it's true.

He doesn't want kids, though. He has made that clear.

"Kids are loud and annoying," he says bluntly, his expression dead serious.

It's not said cruelly; it's just logic.

He knows what peace costs him, and he is not willing to trade it.

There is a wisdom in that I wish more adults had.

When I picture his future, I see him exactly where he wants to be in a small apartment not too far from here (over my garage I am guessing), working a job he loves, surrounded by cats, safe in his rhythms.

I see him laughing on the couch, watching ESPN, texting me pictures of burgers he made at work, his hair a little messy, his eyes bright.

I see a girlfriend sitting beside him, someone who laughs at his movie quotes, listens to his rants about sports, and doesn't mind when he hums through dinner.

That's the thing about Tyler: he's never dreamed small.

His dreams just look different.

They don't stretch into the abstract ideas of college, careers, or far-off cities.

They're anchored in comfort, in loyalty, in the small joys that make up his world.

He wants safety.

He wants belonging.

He wants love.

And isn't that all any of us ever really wants?

When I see him with Lynnlee, I see glimpses of who he will be as a man.

She's his shadow, his echo, his biggest fan.

And he's her biggest cheerleader.

When she starts her body movement exercises, her little jumping rituals that help her regulate, he doesn't join in anymore.

Instead, he stands beside her and chants softly, "Jump. Jump. Jump."

His hands clap in rhythm; his voice is steady and proud.

It's more than encouragement. It's recognition.

It's his way of saying, I see you. I understand."

And she does the same for him.

When he gets overwhelmed, she brings him her fidget toys. When he's pacing, she mirrors his steps until he smiles.

It's an unspoken language for two people who don't need words to belong to each other.

Watching them, I sometimes think about that old word the doctors used: limited.

They were wrong.

There's nothing limited about the way he loves.

Nothing is small about the space he holds for the people he cares about.

Nothing is missing in the way he shows up.

He is, in every sense, full.

Every once in a while, I still think about the binders.

They're both in the attic now, tucked away in plastic bins. I can't quite bring myself to burn them yet. They're part of the story (the paper ghosts of everything we've survived). However, if you ever see me out late at night, sipping coffee and eating Twizzlers by a small plastic-smelling fire, just drive on by. It is me letting go of the fight.

The binders don't define him anymore.

If I ever made a new binder, it would look different.

The tabs would say things like:

"Favorite Cats"

"Best Whataburger Orders"

"Movies That Made Him Laugh So Hard He Fell Off the Couch."

"Family Jokes."

"People Who Love Him."

That would be the real record of progress.

The one that the system never measured.

People ask me if I'm scared of the future.

And maybe I should be.

The world still isn't perfect. There are still barriers, still biases, still days when I see the cracks in the system and feel that familiar fire rise up in me.

But fear isn't what I feel anymore.

What I feel now is something I once thought was out of reach: peace.

Peace in knowing that he is happy.

Peace in knowing that we built a world where he can be exactly who he is.

Peace in knowing that when I'm gone, he won't be alone because his siblings will carry the torch, the same way he carries them.

Jacob will check in on him.

Thomas will make him laugh.

Justin will make sure no one messes with him.

Hailey will call him every day just to say, "Love you, Bub."

Lynnlee will remind him to "jump."

And Harper, loud, unfiltered, full of life, will keep the house noisy enough to make sure he never misses a beat.

He'll still talk to the cats, hum through the afternoons, and narrate life like a sportscaster.

He'll still say "Mom" twenty times a day, even if I can't answer.

Because that's how love works. It echoes.

Sometimes I think back to the beginning of the grocery store meltdowns, the sleepless nights, the doctors with their clipped tones and careful words.

If I could go back, I'd tell that younger version of me something she didn't know yet.

I'd tell her:

You don't have to fix him. You just have to listen.

He'll tell you who he is, maybe not in words, maybe not right away, but he will.

And when he does, it will be the most beautiful sound you've ever heard.

Because now, when I listen, I hear the future.

It sounds like laughter.

It sounds like cats are meowing.

It sounds like the hum of a boy who was never silent, just waiting for the world to quiet down long enough to hear him.

The last chapter isn't really an ending.

It's just the echo of everything we've already lived, still ringing through our home.

And if I've learned anything, it's this:

The world may never understand him completely.

But it doesn't have to.

He understands himself.

He knows what he loves.

He knows who he is.

And that FINALLY is enough.

Epilogue – The Quiet After the Storm

Sometimes I feel like I won a war.

Other days, I feel like the battles will never end.

The fights are still there, just slightly different now.

They don't happen in IEP meetings or sterile classrooms anymore. They happen quietly inside our home.

Sometimes it's a fight to change the sheets because the backup set doesn't feel the same.

Sometimes it's the fight to get dinner right, to make sure the texture of the pasta isn't off, or the sauce doesn't have the wrong kind of tomato bits.

Sometimes I lose those battles.

Some nights, I'm too tired to cook another "safe meal." Work runs late. Someone else needs me. Life doesn't bend just because autism doesn't like surprises. And I watch him settle for a Hungry Man or a salad again, and I feel that familiar sting of failure that never really goes away.

I used to be his voice in the silence, his interpreter, his defender, his advocate, his shield against the world.

Now he fills the quiet with his own voice. Facts about sports. Movie trivia. Reruns of Friends we've seen a hundred times.

We sit together on the couch, quoting the lines before the characters even speak.

He knows every one.

"Could I be wearing any more clothes?" he'll shout, and I laugh because Chandler and Joey taught him sarcasm before I ever could.

It's our new language. Not therapy words. Not scripts. Just shared laughter, built from years of surviving each other's storms.

And in those moments, when I'm not a mother fighting for services or a woman balancing work and kids and exhaustion, I'm just sitting next to my son, laughing at something familiar, something easy.

It's so ordinary; it's sacred.

Because this is the part no one prepares you for, the after.

After the diagnosis.

After the therapy.

After the reports, goals, benchmarks, and endless paperwork.

After you've fought every fight worth fighting.

The world quiets down, but your heart doesn't.

You still listen for the signs, still brace for the meltdowns, still hold your breath when the phone rings from a number you don't recognize.

You learn that peace doesn't mean the war is over. It just means you've learned how to live between the battles.

And honestly, I think that's what growth really is: learning to live in the in-between.

When I look at him now, this grown man who once couldn't stand to be touched, who now hugs me every night before bed, I feel every version of him layered together.

The silent baby.

The jumping boy.

The teenager is learning about a world that didn't always make sense.

The man who talks to cats and cheers for his sister and still eats the same lunch every day.

All of them still live here.

And I still live here too, somewhere between relief and exhaustion, between laughter and fear, between knowing we made it and knowing we will always be learning how to keep making it.

But when I watch him quote Friends or talk to Oreo or chant "jump, jump, jump" for Lynnlee, I know something I didn't know before:

We didn't just survive.

We built something that lasts.

We built a life.

And even if the battles keep coming, even if the sheets feel wrong, or dinner's late, or the world still stares, sometimes we've already won the only war that ever mattered.

He's here. He's happy. He's himself. And that's enough.

For the Mothers Who Came Before the Hashtags

For the mothers who fought before there were Facebook groups or podcasts,

before the checklists and color-coded plans,

before "neurodiversity" became a word people knew how to say.

For the ones who filled binders instead of journals.

Who learned the law between loads of laundry.

Who cried in parking lots and still showed up the next morning with coffee and determination.

For the parents who were told their children were broken,

and who refused to believe it.

For the fathers who sat through meetings and bit their tongues,

for the siblings who became protectors too soon,

for the grandparents who kept the door open even when they didn't understand.

For the teachers who listened.

For the doctors who didn't.

For the therapists who saw potential instead of prognosis.

For every family that has ever had to make the world softer,

room by room, light by light, day by day.

For every child who was ever called "too much," and every parent who whispered, "You're perfect as you are."

This book is for you.

For the battles you have won, the ones you're still fighting,

and the quiet victories no one else ever sees.

And most of all, for the kids, like Tyler, who never needed fixing, only understanding.

Because before the hashtags and awareness months, before the ribbons and research, there was just love: loud, stubborn, inconvenient, and miraculous.

And that's still enough to change the world.

From Tyler

From Tyler

Hey world this is Tyler Hinkle. My favorite SportsCenter anchor is Jay Harris. Here are some clues why he is my favorite anchor.

1. 1.He joined ESPN in 2003
2. 2. He was the 6pm eastern anchor along with Brian Kenny.
3. 3. He worked with John Anderson, Hannah Storm, Brian Kenny, David Lloyd, Neil Evvert, and Kevin Connors.
4. 4. Him and Hannah Storm are great friends

That's what I like about Jay Harris.

www.ingramcontent.com/pod-product-compliance
Lightning Source LLC
Chambersburg PA
CBHW072116300726
48975CB00003B/832